WENDY KREMER

THE
POTTERY
PROJECT

Complete and Unabridged

LINFORD
Leicester

First published in Great Britain in 2017

First Linford Edition
published 2018

A catalogue record for this book is available
from the British Library.

ISBN 978–1–4448–3580–9

Published by
F. A. Thorpe (Publishing)
Anstey, Leicestershire

Set by Words & Graphics Ltd.
Anstey, Leicestershire
Printed and bound in Great Britain by
T. J. International Ltd., Padstow, Cornwall

This book is printed on acid-free paper

THE POTTERY PROJECT

Commissioned to assess the Midland Pottery Company's financial prospects, Craig Baines faces an angry manager — Sharon Vaughan has had no warning of his arrival. The workforce soon accepts their well-meaning visitor, even though they know his findings could result in dismissals. When Craig detects that someone is pinching china and pitches in with Sharon to help solve the crime, she becomes increasingly aware of her attraction to him. But after his report is complete and he's about to leave, has she left it too late to let him know?

1

Sharon viewed the visitor dubiously and commented bluntly, 'You've been commissioned to examine the Midland Pottery Company's activities? The chairman hired you?' Studying his expression, she decided he might be telling the truth and, unknown to her, Granville had engaged him. Feeling irritated, she continued, 'Is this because the company's not doing very well so far this year? Well, it's temporary! Every firm has its ups and downs. If the board is dissatisfied, it could have asked me to explain our present situation.'

It looked like she hadn't known he was coming. He noted her increased colour and tried to sound sympathetic. 'I don't intend to push anyone around, or interfere. I'm just going to collect data so that I can make suggestions about keeping the company on track.

My job is to analyse the situation.' He shrugged his broad shoulders. 'It's up to the owners whether they take my advice or not. I understand your annoyance if you weren't expecting me; and fluctuating profit is normal in every firm, but a company needs to make a regular profit to secure its long-term survival. It's very hard to turn things around once the rot sets in.'

Even these days, it was unusual to find that a woman was managing a company. Craig was pleasantly surprised to find that this one was young, fairly tall, slim, and with a mass of rich auburn hair that framed a very attractive face.

She tossed her head and glared at him. 'We *are* making a profit!'

Sounding annoyingly patient, he replied, 'Miss Vaughan, the first year you didn't, and the second and third years were quite good, but since then you've barely cut even. From my preliminary study, I notice you also have very little cash in reserve. That's

2

always extremely risky. At times, an outsider sees the situation clearer. I'm trained to suggest sensible moves that improve prospects.' He paused. 'I'm used to opposition, and I understand why people do battle, but I'll ignore any protests and get on with my work, with or without your help. I'm responsible to the company owners and not to you, Miss Vaughan.'

She took a deep breath and folded her arms across her chest. 'And why wasn't I informed of your arrival?'

Craig viewed her angry brown eyes. They were speckled with touches of amber. He shrugged. 'I suspect they didn't want to face your disapproval, and ducked! They presented you with a fait accompli because it was easier than discussing it with you first. The board is quite entitled to do so.'

Sharon replied heatedly, 'I imagine your services are expensive; and as you rightly remark, we don't have huge financial reserves. Why waste money on you, when we need it for more urgent things?'

'Because it's a sensible long-term move. It improves your chances of survival.'

She straightened. 'We're not on the brink of economic failure, Mr Baines!'

He tried to sound sympathetic but didn't realize that annoyed her even more. 'Not at present, but it could happen. I'm here to help prevent it.' He met her glance. 'Perhaps employing me does seem an unnecessary expense, but your board is facing reality. Perhaps I'll conclude that everything is viable and the prospects are rosy. But on the other hand, I may suggest sensible adjustments. Instead of getting all het up, why don't you save us both a lot of hassle? I'm afraid you've no choice.'

She stared at him silently for a second. A devilish look came into his eyes and his mouth twitched. She turned on her heel and marched out, passing through the main office with heightened colour and a clatter down the metal stairway. Craig watched her, and amusement flickered.

The soft folds of his overcoat fell into place when he stood up. He grabbed his briefcase and decided to try to find someone who was friendlier. If Miss Vaughan remained as hostile as she was this minute, he was facing a hard time.

He'd try to settle in before she returned. He sauntered into the outer office. The lady who'd dealt with him on arrival was busy behind her desk. Craig could tell she'd be more forthcoming than Miss Vaughan. She smiled at him, and he smiled back.

Sharon had rushed past in a tizzy without explanations, and left her to deal with him. Gaynor couldn't guess why he was here, but she'd be accommodating until Sharon clarified the situation. She examined the visitor more closely and noted he was a well-dressed, tall, good-looking man with grey eyes and coal-black hair. He also had a winning smile and a polite manner.

'Hello again!' he greeted her. 'You're . . . ?'

5

'Gaynor, Gaynor Jenkins. I'm Sharon's . . . Miss Vaughan's assistant.'

'And I'm Craig Baines.' He held out his hand and Gaynor shook it. 'I'm going to be around for several weeks, Gaynor. I need somewhere with an internet connection. I don't mind if it's a broom cupboard in the corner, or twenty square feet of open space. I don't need filing cabinets, a coffee machine, or any other paraphernalia, just a desk and an internet link.' He smiled hopefully.

'Has Miss Vaughan given her permission?'

'To be quite honest, no, not yet. I presume she's trying to clarify the situation at this moment. But I can assure you that the chairman, Mr Jackson, and the other board members have given me the go-ahead.' He smiled again and tilted his head to one side. 'Perhaps I should explain why I'm here? I'm checking the company's financial standing. I'm not intending to do anyone out of a job, or to turn things upside down. I'm just going to collect facts and make suggestions. It's up to the board of directors what they do with my findings. I'm not your enemy. I'm just doing my job, like you're doing yours, and I'll be eternally grateful if you co-operate and help.'

Gaynor felt her resistance fading fast. She nodded. 'So you're a . . . ?'

'I'm what they call an actuary. It's a fancy name for someone who figures out the financial impacts, risks, or any other possible dangers in a company's makeup.'

'Oh! I see.' She fiddled with the papers on her desk. 'I suppose if Mr Jackson and the others have approved, we'll have to co-operate. There's a small cubicle over there with an internet connection. Will that suit?' She pointed in the appropriate direction. 'We used to keep the printer in there because it was so loud, but we don't anymore — the modern ones are much quieter. We've never used the internet connection, but it was installed when the offices were renovated. I've tried it and it does work.'

'That sounds perfect.'

Gaynor asked curiously, 'From the way Sharon took off, I gather she doesn't approve?'

He grinned. 'You presume correctly.' He shrugged. 'But until I get my official marching orders from the company owners, I'm afraid that Miss Vaughan will have to put up with me whether she likes it or not.'

Loyally she declared, 'Sharon is a good boss; fair. Everyone likes her.'

'I expect she is! She wouldn't be managing this company if she couldn't handle employees. It makes no difference to me whether she co-operates or not. I'm here to do my job, and I have permission to gather the statistics I need. I'll get out from under everyone's feet as fast as I can. Oh, I'll need the passwords for the computer, and I'd be grateful for any information about how the china is produced, or that'll give me a better insight into the terminology.'

Gaynor nodded. 'We have various old catalogues and flyers that explain the process in simple terms. I'll wait until Sharon comes back and gives me permission about the passwords, if you don't mind.'

Craig nodded. 'Of course. I understand.'

'Would you like a cup of coffee?'

'Love one!'

Over coffee they chatted, and Craig found Gaynor was married with two teenage sons and that her husband worked for a local gas company. Craig could tell Gaynor identified herself with her job, and she also mentioned most of the employees were very loyal to the company. That was a positive sign, but it could be problematic if his findings suggested dismissals might be a deciding factor sometime in the future.

Gaynor started to search for the brochures he wanted. He noticed she pulled a piece of paper with various letters and numbers out of the top drawer and put it down on the desk while continuing to search. He wondered if they were passwords. He frowned but didn't comment.

Gaynor asked. 'Are you married? Children?'

'No, I'm on the move a lot. I haven't had much time to think seriously about marriage or children.' He winked. 'Not that I scorn the idea. One day perhaps.'

Gaynor liked him. There was something congenial and friendly in his smile, and the expression in his grey eyes told her he was caring, even though he was doing a job that might have negative consequences for them all. 'When you meet the right one, that'll change fast. My Ken and I weren't looking either, and now we have two strapping boys and a big mortgage!'

The telephone interrupted their tête-à-tête. Craig left her and went to inspect his allotted pigeonhole; it satisfied his needs. There was no window. The desk and chair took up seventy percent of the space. He spotted a hook on one of the walls and took off his coat. The wall separating the room from Gaynor's office had half-windows. He was glad that he'd be autonomous. From past experience, he knew that a barrier between him and everyone else made things easier all round. He hoped people would soon accept his presence and stop thinking he was a monster with two heads.

Craig knew that his boss had spotted his strong points straight away at his interview — he had a sharp analytical brain and a basically friendly attitude. Some of his colleagues found it hard to accept they weren't popular, and others had difficulties communicating with people. Most of them worked permanently in the headquarters of banks, insurance companies and health insurers.

Craig enjoyed moving from company to company. As long as he was single, it presented no problem. Sometimes he worked in middle-sized companies, and other times smaller firms like this one.

He recalled the basic information he'd gathered about Midland Potteries Co. Ltd. from the internet. Turnover: £5 million, producing chinaware, 85 employees, located in the Midlands, founded in 2012. He added under his breath as his brain whizzed through the information again, 'And with a manageress who breathes fire.'

* * *

'Granville, why did you engage this man without discussing it with me first?'

Granville viewed Sharon with increasing dismay. He'd guessed that she'd be annoyed, but he'd hoped her irritation would have lessened by the time she reached him. He ran his fingers through his hair; blond strands fell back onto his forehead in a tidy tuft. 'Steady on, Sharon! You've got the wrong end of the stick. It's nothing personal, just business. A company owner I met at the club told me how this firm had sorted them out. His business was going downhill fast at the time, and they improved things no end. I mentioned it to the others recently, and after considering our present position, we all thought it might be a good idea to employ them.'

'The pottery isn't going downhill!'

'No, but you must admit last year wasn't good, and this year we're stagnating. Everyone agreed it was a good idea.'

Eyes still blazing, she commented, 'I wish you'd told me what you were doing. I should have been forewarned. People like this man usually suggest throwing employees out onto the street.'

'Oh, come off it! You're jumping to conclusions. Last time we talked about the pottery, you said yourself that we aren't doing as well as expected. I don't want anyone to lose their job, but it's foolish to ignore tendencies and throw good money after bad. We're not in it for fun.' He straightened his tweed jacket and wiped his hand on his corduroy trousers. 'When we first met, you convinced me the company was worth buying and it would make a profit; it has done quite well. If we get someone in to analyse the situation, it doesn't automatically mean dismissals.'

Sharon managed to relax a little and converse more rationally. The dice were thrown; protest was pointless. She'd rushed out without her coat. Her muted moss-coloured wool dress was warm; but unless there was a roaring fire in the grate, Granville's sitting room was never cosy, and at the moment the outsized fireplace was empty. She hugged herself. 'I just wish you'd told me before you employed someone who's going to cause disruption in the firm.'

Granville took her shoulders. 'Sharon, he won't cause disruption. My friend told me he was very discreet, and the final suggestions he made were spot on. You do your job brilliantly; but it won't do any harm for an outsider to take a look at things, will it?'

Sharon felt committed to the company and the people who worked there, but she also admitted Granville was only being sensible. Their good working relationship had become personal recently, and they'd gone out often in the last couple of months. Sharon guessed that he liked her a great deal and, provided she gave him the right signals, he might even want something more serious. She'd managed to sidetrack him, but she didn't intend to playact and pretend she liked him more than she did. She didn't like some of his friends; and she was too independent, and enjoyed her work too much, to ever want to give it all up to live like a bird in a golden cage.

Granville originated from a family going back over several generations. They had started off working a small farmstead, and invested their growing wealth in the wool trade and later in weaving mills during the Industrial

Revolution. Their social standing had increased with their riches, and their earnings had been cleverly invested in property and other lucrative ventures. Up to the present, those investments had enabled the Jackson family to live a lifestyle that demanded little effort on its part.

It hadn't corrupted him. Granville wasn't conceited or arrogant. He was nice, and Sharon liked him; but liking wasn't enough for anything binding. Her feelings had a lot to do with his character. Generally he sat back and let others take the decisions and the responsibility. His contribution to running the pottery consisted of merely attending board meetings. He was their chairman, but he was also on the board of several other companies. It wasn't characteristic of him to hire someone without consulting her first. She looked up into his pale blue eyes. He had an interesting face, ash-blond hair, and a ruddy complexion demonstrating how often he was outdoors. She repeated softly, 'I wish you'd tipped me off.'

He leaned forward and kissed her forehead. 'I know, but we took a spontaneous decision and I didn't think he'd be here so fast. Apparently another company went bust just before this chap was due to arrive, so he had a gap in his schedule. His boss contacted me on Sunday and asked whether he could come this week. I intended to phone you, but I went to a horse show in Chester yesterday, forgot about it when I got home, and when I was about to phone you this morning Charlie Hawkins came round with a new thoroughbred for my stables. It pushed everything else out of my mind. He's a beauty. You must take a look at him next time round.' He looked at his watch. 'Look, I appreciate why you're a bit annoyed, but it's for the best, old girl. Let him scrutinize and inspect, show him whatever he wants to see, and do what you can to help him, please! You may be pleasantly surprised. Perhaps he'll

17

come up with some sensible suggestions to improve prospects.' He
checked his watch again. 'I've got to
throw you out, I'm afraid. I'm due for
a round of golf in half an hour, and I
still have to change and drive there.'

Sharon sighed. There was no point in
harassing him. Perhaps she should be
pleased that he was taking any kind of
interest in the firm. He hadn't so far,
apart from religiously attending the
board meetings. Even then, he'd never
studied the figures or thought about an
answer to any of the problems she'd
forewarned him about. She threaded
her fingers through her hair. 'Okay, I'll
try: I don't like it, and I'm still not
convinced he's worth the expense, but
you are chairman — and as I presume
the others are behind you, there's no
point in arguing any longer.'

'Good girl!'

'Don't expect me to like him, though,
because I won't.'

He relaxed measurably. 'I hope not.
Off you go! Back to the grindstone and

Mr Baines. He's a decent chap actually, when you get to know him. I talked to him briefly in London.'

Outside Granville's sprawling mansion, Sharon sat in her Mini and stared across the neat gardens and greenery surrounding the house. Resigning herself to helping Craig Baines, she straightened, then started the engine and drove back to the pottery. She felt decidedly calmer than when she'd left. She drove into the yard and parked neatly on the side. The company buildings were a mixture of new and old.

She was reconciled to the inevitable as she passed the kilns and the mass of raw forms waiting for the first firing. She ran her eye over the plates and bowls being formed by jiggering, and the more irregular forms of items lined up in their plaster moulds. Going through the adjoining workshop and acknowledging anyone who noticed her, she crossed to another room where women were busy painting the bone china. Sharon never failed to admire how skilled and talented they were. Finally, she reached the storage and packing area and climbed the adjoining metal stairway to the offices under the roof. She steeled herself to meet Mr Craig Baines again and decided to get it over with straight away.

A quick glance around showed her he was already settled in the corner cubbyhole. The door was closed and he was busy. He didn't look up.

Gaynor fluffed her hair into place and shrugged. 'I didn't know what to do with him. He told me he was authorized to be here and wanted somewhere out of the way. He didn't mind that it's a pokey little room.'

Sharon nodded. 'That's okay. I checked with Granville. It looks like the board arranged to employ him and forgot to tell us. He came sooner than originally planned too, and Granville didn't warn me beforehand.'

Gaynor sniffed. 'It's odd that he

forgot something so important, something that affects you directly. I don't know why you stand him, even though he owns most of the company.'

Sharon thrust her hands into her pockets. 'Granville's okay. Now and then he gets his priorities mixed up, but I've worked for worse bosses. Some want to interfere all the time. He's never done that.'

Gaynor took a sheet of paper from the photocopier. 'Undoubtedly because he doesn't have a clue what's going on!'

Sharon spluttered and answered, 'You're right, but don't tell anyone! He's perfectly entitled to watch from afar and take his share of the profits.'

'Huh! He was born into money and does nothing to deserve what he takes from us.'

Sharon decided not to persevere with the conversation. Gaynor didn't approve of her seeing Granville outside office hours. She never ceased to warn her they weren't suited. Sharon asked, 'Anything important in the post?'

'No, nothing special. One order came in via the website. I was just about to pass it to Frank so that he deals with it as soon as possible.'

'Do that. I'd better make my peace with Mr Baines. It looks like he'll be around for a while, so I may as well bury the hatchet.'

Gaynor set off with the order, and Sharon went to see Craig Baines. He was seated and busy with his laptop on the desk. She knocked briefly and went in. He looked up, and she felt her colour heighten.

Craig mused that somehow she managed to look regal. Her thick hair was well cut and hung loose to her shoulders. Her mouth had a resolute set to it.

Sharon forced lightness into her voice. 'It seems you're expected, but no one bothered to inform me. Now that I've cleared that point, I'll give you as much help as I can. I'm just going to ask you not to harass the staff in any way, and to let me know what's in your final prognosis so that I'm forewarned about the outcome. I'm the one who has to face the board, and I'd like a little time to study your findings, whether they're good or bad.'

He smiled briefly with no trace of animosity. Sharon was grateful for that. 'As long as the board has no objections! I'll mention it next time I talk to someone in charge. I don't think anyone will object to you reading about the company's prospects as soon as I have a fair idea. It won't change anything if you get an earlier insight.'

Sharon relaxed slightly. He was here to do his job. Clearly he was used to facing hostile receptions wherever he went.

His pleasant deep voice jogged her concentration again. 'It would be a great help to have the passwords for the various departments. I notice that you only allow access to computer information to pertinent people in each section. That's good for confidentiality, but makes my job more difficult because I have to co-ordinate statistics and need access to the whole system.' He waited and considered her expression for a while before he successfully disarmed her with a smile.

Sharon wasn't blind to his attractions; but if he thought he could wrap her round his finger in that way, he was wrong. His compelling grey eyes and firm features, and the confident set of his shoulders, were impressive. Unconsciously her brow furrowed. 'Okay, I'll give you a list. Gaynor and I are the only ones with overall access. It goes without saying that I want to keep it that way. I expect that you'll never reveal any sensitive information to anyone else.' She glanced round. 'It's a bit cramped in here, but Gaynor told me you don't mind.'

His eyes twinkled and he gestured round. 'This is all I need, and a cup of coffee now and then.'

She ignored the unexplainable tingle of excitement as their eyes locked.

24

'Right! I'll get on with my work. If you need anything else . . . '

'I'll ask. Oh, while you're here — I've glanced at past and present catalogues. I presume the items on offer are updated regularly on the website?'

She pushed her hair back off her temples and was glad to concentrate on work. 'It's changed from time to time. The website shows our best sellers straight off, but people can surf through and see everything we have on offer.'

'Such as?'

'We started by producing individual pieces of pottery with people's names on it. You know the kind of thing — a gift for Mother's Day, for a wedding, Christmas, that sort of thing. We sold, and still sell, large amounts of those to firms, individuals and other groups. A little later we started making complete services, and one of our first is still extremely popular. Perhaps you've seen it? In pale green and yellow, with chickens and the vague shape of a country cottage in the background?'

He nodded. 'I think my sister-in-law has a set.'

'We were a mere handful of people in the beginning, with one kiln — the only one that was still in decent working order. The others were repaired as sales picked up. Now we've started to replace them with more modern versions. They're more efficient and need less energy. Luckily the area around here already had a strong tradition in making pottery, and we found people who were skilled in the profession quite easily.'

'You and Gaynor run the management side?'

'Yes, we cope very well between us. Gaynor has been here from day one. The rest of the staff is made up of potters, painters, kiln workers, warehouse, and logistics workers.'

'And you're local? Do you come from a pottery background?'

'No, but when I read about the pottery it sounded just right for me. It's a challenge, but we produce beautiful and useful end products.'

'Okay, that gives me a bit of an insight. In case I come up against any difficulties . . . '

'Just ask.'

'Good. And please remember, I'm not here to harass anyone. I'm doing a job. Perhaps I'll be more useful than you think.' He held out his hand. His eyes were quick with mischief. 'As we'll be working closely for the next couple of weeks, I'm Craig — and you're . . . ?'

Her skin grew hot and cold and her stomach tightened. She took his hand briefly. It felt warm and pleasant. 'Sharon,' she said.

2

Sharon didn't see very much of Craig once he began his work. He spent most of the time bent over his laptop and surrounded by papers. Gaynor supplied her with titbits of information about him. She enlightened Sharon that he was staying with Mildred Hardwick and her husband. They ran the only pub in the village, and let out rooms to the occasional visitor. He didn't seem to cause much disturbance in the pottery. People already knew why he was there. Sharon was always surprised how quickly they figured out what was going on.

Craig visited the production sheds, the firing section, and the other units to study things. Sharon tried to avoid him as much as she could, but she often saw him talking to one of the workers. She wasn't surprised to notice how much curiosity and interest he created, especially among the female workers. His appearance and background made him an exotic figure among local inhabitants. His clothes were expensive, he was good-looking, and people soon decided he was also 'very brainy'.

Gaynor added, 'After his evening meal at the pub, he often joins a game of darts and pays for his share of rounds. People like him because he doesn't act like a smart aleck, although they all know he's clever. The female population have noticed him too. Sandra is throwing blatant signals in his direction. He hasn't responded yet, but it'll be interesting to see whether he shows any interest before he leaves. Someone told me Rhonda has been making excuses to bump into him in the village too. It must be a strange life though. Moving from place to place doesn't give him much chance to make real friends.'

Any reservations Gaynor had defi- nitely melted away after Craig spontaneously offered to give her oldest boy some extra coaching in maths. She told Sharon. 'Gary told us afterwards that Craig was 'real cool', and made it easy for him to see where he was going wrong.'

Sharon was pleased for Gaynor, but felt a little irritated by how fast he'd ingratiated himself into the community. She mused that people were ignoring the possibility that he could ultimately be responsible for job losses.

Ruffling the papers in front of her, Sharon felt obliged to comment. 'Since Sandra is our local version of Scarlett Johansson, I'm not surprised to hear that that she's trying her luck. With her blond hair, curvy figure, and blue come-hither eyes, who could blame any man? But it's a pity she doesn't pay more attention to grooming and not just rely on her looks. She always has laddered stockings, have you noticed? He comes from down south. That's a more sophisticated background, where women are stylish. Even though Sandra is extremely attractive, he'll notice laddered stockings and sloppy grooming.'

Gaynor shrugged and muttered, 'Not if he's just looking for a fling. I don't honestly think Sandra is holding out for a wedding ring either. She just wants some extra excitement.'

'Yes, I expect you're right.'

'What are you planning this weekend? Ken and I were thinking of going to Wednesbury's Art Gallery on Sunday. You're welcome to come with us. There's an art exhibition on at the moment. When I mention the word 'art', Ken won't need persuading. I'm positive the boys won't come. They don't want to go anywhere with Mum and Dad anymore.'

Sharon smiled at her and her eyes twinkled. 'Well, Ken does paint lovely landscapes these days. When he first started to go to evening classes, the results left much to be desired, but he's improved a great deal since then. He's painting really nice local scenes these days. You should encourage him.'

'Oh, I do! I know how much he enjoys his hobby. My problem is to work out where to hang all the stuff when he's finished. It would hurt his feelings if I didn't put it up on the wall. We even have pictures in the toilet!'

Sharon chuckled. 'Why not suggest, very gently, that he could contribute some of his pictures to a local jumble sale or charity do? He'd be doing a good deed and making some room for new paintings.'

'Hmm! That's a great suggestion, but it'd be better for someone like you to suggest it. You're good at that sort of thing. People don't realize you've manipulated them until it's too late. Well . . . how about Sunday?'

'I can't, I'm afraid. Granville is hosting a social get-together and I've promised to go.'

'Ah well! What about the following Sunday? We could combine a visit with a walk afterwards. Ken could take some inspirational photos for future paintings.'

'Sounds good! See how Ken feels. If it's still on, I'll come.'

The telephone rang in the outer office. Gaynor smiled and nodded. 'Never a moment's peace! I'll let you know.'

Sharon got up and grabbed her bag. 'And I'm off to sort out that company that sent us the wrong paint. I'll take their original shipment with me so that they can't argue. There's no point in trying to sort it out over the phone. They just won't accept they've made a mistake.'

Gaynor led the way and Sharon followed. She noticed Craig wasn't in his office. She found him in the painting room, chatting to Sandra. Sandra's tight pink overall emphasised her small waist, enticing bust and shapely hips.

Without interrupting them, she passed and went to the shelves to get two large tins of paint. She chatted briefly to one of the other painters on her way back. She had no intention of asking Craig what he was doing there.

'Morning, Sharon!'

She replied through stiff lips, 'Hello!' She looked across and reminded herself that he was merely passing through. For some reason she was disconcerted. She tried to avoid him, but was still much too interested, and it didn't seem to make much difference if she met him or not. She was half in anticipation and half in dread. He wasn't just good-looking; he was intelligent too. But he was also a rolling stone that gathered no moss. She couldn't forget the fact that he was here to find the company's weaknesses — *her* weaknesses. Others didn't worry about what would be in his final report.

He had the look of a man who'd always get what he wanted, and at the moment there was a trace of laughter in his voice. 'Sandra was just explaining what she does. I must admit, the whole process is a lot more interesting than I expected. I never thought about how china was made before now, but this has given me a real insight. I don't think I'll ever lift another mug without thinking about the work that's gone into its making.'

Sharon looked at them and responded unemotionally. 'Sandra is one of our best painters. She's been with us for over two years.' Sharon was not as relaxed as she seemed, and Sharon reminded herself that she was the manager; this man was just passing through. As casually as she could manage, she declared, 'I must be off. I'm hoping to catch one of our suppliers before he closes for the weekend.'

Sandra was giving Craig all her attention. He nodded and replied, 'Have a good weekend! See you Monday?'

Sharon hoisted her bag and picked up the tins. 'Yes, I expect so. Bye, Sandra!'

Without looking at her, Sandra responded, 'Bye!'

Sharon was glad to leave. Gaynor's

recent comments about Sandra flirting with him were still fresh in her mind. She told herself she didn't care what Mr Craig Baines did in his spare time or if he was flirting with one of their employees during working hours. There was no law against it, and no doubt Sandra would welcome his attentions.

Out in the yard, Sharon started the engine and reversed carefully onto the road. She looked briefly at her watch and concentrated on travelling via the fastest route to the suppliers. On Friday the roads were often extremely busy. Now and then, as she negotiated her way via various shortcuts, the picture of Craig Baines and Sandra laughing together whizzed through her brain. She just hoped the woman didn't disclose any sensitive company information to him.

⋆   ⋆   ⋆

Sharon got out of her Mini and viewed Granville's house for a short time. It was over two hundred years old. The family had aimed for the stars and, even though money was no object, somehow the final result was disappointing. It sprawled and was unwelcoming in appearance. There were too many buttresses and shadows everywhere.

She glanced at the conventional garden, with its ornamental bushes, and further into the distance where footpaths ran across the fields. Soft breezes mussed her hair. The morning mist had lifted and the air was fresh and cool. Nearby, the leaves of the trees rustled in the breeze, and birds were busy tossing the ones on the ground aside to search underneath them for food. The house itself was half a mile from the main road. Looking down the long tree-bordered drive, she could see the open cast-iron gates and wondered if the surrounding properties and farms belonged to Granville's family too. To the rear of the house was an area of woodland, and the front faced the ornamental gardens and the countryside beyond. The garden had been planted to impress and not to merge with the rural surroundings.

Sharon walked along a gravelled pathway that circumnavigated the house. There was a single flowerbed bordering the front. Halfway along, some shallow steps led up to a portico and the main entrance.

She straightened her knee-length skirt and buttoned its matching jacket. Being careful not to scrape her heels on the sharp-edged gravel, she reached the entrance and was pleased to see their local GP and his wife just about to go in. She joined them.

After the usual greetings, she followed them into a cloakroom where the hooks were already full. She waited for them to deposit their coats. Julie Smallwood smiled. 'How are you? I haven't seen you since the meeting about saving the church tower, and that was months ago.'

They walked towards the sitting

room. 'I'm fine. Yes, it has been a while since we last saw each other. How are you? How's the campaign going?'

'It's flagging, but we'll get there one day. Thank you for volunteering to help with the posters. I'll get back to you about them when things have been sorted out. I'm doing my best to stir things up, but I'm beginning to think that most of the committee simply come to argue.'

Her husband, walking alongside, looked at his wife and chortled. 'Luckily it doesn't stop Julie!'

Sharon enquired, 'Have you asked Granville for a contribution yet? If you haven't, corner him today. Some of his family are buried in the church. You should remind him about that.'

Julie smiled at her. 'Oh yes, I'd forgotten that completely! A perfect reason to make subtle demands. Granville is very willing to support anything to do with the family.'

A buzz of conversation reached them as they entered the room. They stood watching, and then Julie looked at Sharon. 'I was surprised the other day when someone asked me whether or not you and Granville would be naming the day soon.'

Sharon coloured. 'Did they? We're good friends, but nothing more.'

Julie nodded, and her husband lifted his brows before he left them to make his way to a side-table where a waiter was serving drinks. Julie continued, 'I never had the impression that Granville was the love of your life, but he's a good catch. Anyone who marries him will have a full social life, and never need to worry about money.'

Sharon wasn't sure if Julie was teasing or being critical. She certainly didn't like the idea that people were gossiping about her. She commented, 'There's more to marriage than money.'

Julie looked at her carefully. 'You're perfectly right. You can't buy happiness. Ah! James has managed to get us something to drink, and Granville's with him.'

The two men reached them. James was juggling with three long-stemmed crystal glasses, and Granville was in high spirits. He bent and kissed Sharon's cheek, and smiled at the doctor and his wife. 'Glad you could make it. Help yourself to whatever you like. There's a buffet on the other side of the room. I see that you've already found the drinks. You can't see where anything is in this crush. Cheers!'

Julie, Sharon and James lifted their glasses in Granville's direction and took a sip. After a few minutes of pleasantries, Granville slipped his hand under Sharon's elbow. 'I'm going to hijack Sharon. See you later!'

Sharon felt uncomfortable. She was recalling Julie's words, and could understand why gossip was inevitable as soon as people noticed she was seeing Granville regularly. As he steered her across the room, she decided to face reality. She never felt excitement or exhilaration when she was with him. Although she had never been deeply in love with anyone, and wasn't able to compare, she still knew love ought to be special. She wouldn't compromise and drift into a second-best situation. Granville exchanged a few words with the people they passed, and Sharon had to admit he didn't put a foot wrong. He was a social tiger. This wasn't the right moment to sort it out, but it should be soon.

He led her into the Victorian conservatory. Even on a chilly day like today, it still managed to be a lot warmer than anywhere else in the house. Opulent greenery and flowering plants stood in pots and containers among the comfortable wicker-ware chairs and tables. They added a cheerful splash of colour.

He held her at arm's length. 'You look very smart today.'

'Thanks.' Eyeing his double-breasted navy-blue pinstriped suit and bright white shirt, she commented, 'And so do you.'

He smiled. 'I'd rather be in more

comfortable gear and have you to myself, but from time to time I'm obligated to entertain friends and acquaintances.'

Sharon wondered whether he did feel anything special for her. He'd never told her so. Perhaps he was just drifting, too, and looking for someone who fitted his lifestyle. She knew that he thought she was intelligent and looked good. Those were possibly his minimum requirements.

The pottery company, under a previous name, had gone bankrupt through bad management. She had been looking for a job at the time, and read an interview with local dignitaries about what effect the closure would have on the community. She'd studied its prospects, contacted Granville and the others, and convinced them that the pottery could earn money when properly managed. A handful of them had invested their money and bought the bankrupt company for next to nothing. It had paid off. Sharon even owned some of the shares herself.

She'd drifted into accepting Granville's invitations because she'd no other boyfriend and little time to meet anyone new. She enjoyed his company. He was thoughtful and attentive, but she wasn't thinking along serious lines.

The local vicar, his wife, and his teenage daughter came in and interrupted any further conversation. Sharon was glad of the disturbance. Vicar Walters had a domed head and kind, inquisitive eyes. His movements were brisk, and he listened meticulously to people's problems. His clothes hung loosely on his hunched body. His wife had curly grey hair that she kept under control with a weekly visit to the local hairdresser's, where she picked up village gossip. She passed it all on to her husband at lunch the same day. She was busily involved in all parish affairs, and ran committees and meetings with an iron fist. Their daughter Gloria was small and dark, with her hair tied into a thick ponytail. Sharon had rarely spoken to her; somehow she always looked jumpy and uncomfortable.

Sharon wasn't a regular churchgoer. She smiled anyway as Granville politely drew the vicar and his wife into conversation about the conservatory and explained how much care and attention the wrought-iron construction demanded.

Vicar Walters nodded. 'I expect it does, but it's worth it. You can't compare something like this to the plastic constructions they sell these days.'

'You're right. The whole house is a never-ending drain on resources, but anything of a certain age needs care and attention to preserve it for the next generation.'

The vicar nodded and looked thoughtfully at Sharon, who was glad when Granville turned his attention to Gloria. 'What are you doing these days, Gloria?'

Gloria opened her mouth, but her mother was faster. 'Gloria is studying at the local college. She'll finish her teacher training next year, and then we'll find her a job locally.' She eyed Granville determinedly. 'You need the right connections, but I hope we'll be lucky.'

Gloria fiddled with a fold in her skirt. Sharon could see that she felt uncomfortable. There was no one else in her age group present. Sharon considered the mother's determined expression and guessed why. She was hoping to bring Gloria to the notice of the 'right kind of people' as early as possible.

The vicar declared, 'I've heard about your wonderful library, Granville. Any chance of a peep?'

With a rueful glance in Sharon's direction, he answered, 'Of course. Come with me; I'll show you around. There are shelves and shelves of books. I bet some of them haven't been moved since the day they were put there. I think a lot of them were bought for appearances' sake.'

The vicar's wife gushed, 'That's the

privilege of having money to spare. It sounds interesting. You may have real treasures hidden among them. I'd love to come too — assuming that you won't mind, Granville? What about you, Gloria? Coming?'

Gloria remained silent, and Sharon decided to help. 'She can keep me company.'

Shrugging, Gloria's mother turned away and trailed after the two men.

Sharon was silent at first, and then Gloria stated, 'Thanks. I'm not at all interested in books or libraries.'

'But you have to be interested in them. Books are part of studies.'

'I just read the ones I have to. I'm not the least bit passionate about books like my parents are.'

'It sounds like you're not looking forward to a career as a teacher very much, either.'

Sensing that she could be truthful, Gloria fiddled with a fold in her skirt again. 'No, not much.'

'Then why are you studying?'

Gloria shrugged. 'I don't know. My parents decided what was best for me, and I fell in line. It's easier than arguing with them. I can never win.'

'Haven't you ever thought about what *you'd* like to do?'

She shrugged and nodded. 'When I said I wanted to work with animals, my mother called it a silly idea and said they wouldn't support me — that I should learn something sensible!'

'It's none of my business, but surely it's important what you want, not what your mother wants. There are lots of possibilities: vets, zoos, carers, stables, breeding.'

Sounding fed up, Gloria said, 'You don't know my mother. She steamrolls any suggestions I make.'

Sharon was irritated. 'Then you have to put your foot down now, otherwise your mother will be in control forever more. She'll choose your pals, your pastimes, your interests, and you'll end up with no life of your own. Some jobs with animals don't require qualifications, although the ones that do pay more. Why don't you make enquiries? Perhaps there's a vet who needs a secretary — someone who's prepared to help him with the practical side of things too. Dog kennels or animal sanctuaries are often looking for helpers. I don't suppose that you'll earn much without qualifications, but it's important to do something that makes you happy. Money isn't everything.'

The young woman nodded mutely. Sharon decided to give her time to think things over. 'I'm going to get something to drink. Want some? I'll be back in a minute.'

Gloria shook her head and sat down in one of the wicker chairs.

On her return, Sharon stopped in her tracks when she saw Craig Baines sitting next to Gloria. They were chatting, and Sharon noticed how lively Gloria looked. The picture demonstrated to her what an impact Craig Baines made on people without much perceptible effort on his part. He was wearing smart denim jeans with a tweed jacket and a pristine white shirt. He was tanned, something she'd never noticed under the artificial lighting in the company. The extra colour made his grey eyes stand out in his face. He saw her and noted her surprise.

Laughing softly, he pronounced. 'Yes, it's me!'

'What are you doing here?'

'Granville invited me. I escaped into the conservatory to get away from the rest of the guests. Their sole topic of conversation seems to be the last hunt or the next hunt ball. Gloria and I were having a chat about her training and what she'd like to do.' He gave Gloria a smile, and he'd never had a more appreciative audience.

Sharon felt drawn to him in a way that thrilled and frightened her. She was suddenly anxious to escape. 'I understand why you hid. Granville does seem to know a lot of people whose main interests are horses, riding, and gymkhanas.'

He eyed her carefully and she felt her colour rising. 'I wasn't hiding; just avoiding most of the people in there. I didn't think you were the kind of person who belonged to the horsy set.'

'I'm not. I can't even ride. Granville and I are just friends.'

'So I heard.' His voice had a derisive touch to it. Sharon presumed he'd heard the gossip too.

Gloria interrupted, 'Craig just told me that Granville has super stables and a pack of hounds.'

Craig lifted his brows and tilted his head to the side. 'I walked around the garden before I came in.'

Sharon turned to Gloria. 'Yes, he does. The stables are just around the corner. Why don't you take a look? This gathering is undoubtedly very boring for you. It's against the law to hunt for live quarry, but they still organize mock hunts.'

Gloria's eyes lit up. 'Will you tell my

parents where I am when they return?'

'If I see them, yes I will.'

Gloria rushed to the door and disappeared. There was a moment's silence before Craig said, 'I was behind that tropical foliage and heard you talking to Gloria about taking a stand before it's too late.'

Flustered by his presence, Sharon's colour heightened. 'You shouldn't eavesdrop.'

'It wasn't intentional. I made myself comfortable behind the palm trees and the giant cacti long before you arrived with Granville. I decided it'd be easier to keep silent and hidden than pretend I was interested in horsey conversation.' Her eyes sparkled with amusement, and encouraged him to go on. 'I came out to have a tête-à-tête with Gloria when you'd all left.' His eyes twinkled. 'Her parents are quite something, aren't they? He's totally bound up helping other people, and she's busy presiding over every committee within twenty miles of the village. Neither of them seem to have any spare time to give their own daughter a little encouragement.'

'Perhaps they don't realize that she *needs* encouragement. I expect her mother is so used to getting her own way that she really believes she's infallible. I hope Gloria picks up enough courage to do battle before it's too late.'

'I see you've got two glasses of champagne. Can I have one, or do you intend to drink them both?'

She handed him one wordlessly. He lifted his glass in her direction. 'Here's to us, and to the courage of one's convictions.'

Sharon took a sip and searched around for an innocent topic. 'I hear you're staying in the village? Is everything okay?'

'Yes, fine. The landlady is a good cook and the bed's comfortable. Who could ask for more? Do you live in the village?'

'On the edge. I sank all my savings into buying a small run-down cottage.

It's not very big and I'm still modernizing it, bit by bit, but it suits me.'

'You'll find it all a very big change when you move in here.'

She straightened. 'I presume you've been listening to gossip, but I'm not moving anywhere.'

He emptied his glass. 'Then I must've misunderstood things.'

The vicar and his wife came back. Sharon eyed Craig when he turned to face the older woman. His lips parted in a polite smile and a display of straight white teeth. 'Gloria's gone to inspect the stables.'

Gloria's mother tut-tutted. She was visibly pacified when Craig gave her another appealing smile. 'I'm really impressed by Gloria's knowledge about horses, and animals in general,' he said. 'Most teenagers these days don't know a thing unless they ask Google for information via their phones.'

'Yes, Gloria's always been interested in animals. I don't know where she gets it from.'

'Well, she's extremely well-informed. I think you should encourage her to do something professional with all that knowledge, Mrs Walters.'

Sharon had to look away to hide her amusement. She looked at Craig pointedly again before she said goodbye to the vicar and his wife politely, and then left them all to make her way back to the sitting room. She was now looking forward to leaving. She was annoyed to know how widespread the gossip linking her with Granville was. She carried on through the sitting room to the library. Situated on the other side of the house, she was glad to sit there and let the irritation fade. She was particularly annoyed to think that Craig Baines had heard the gossip. It didn't mean anything to him, but he'd heard it and repeated it. Was he trying to annoy her, or just hoping to get confirmation or denial to pass it on to others?

She looked at her watch. On the way back through the hallway, she noticed some people were already leaving, and decided she'd join them. She found Granville with some of his golf cronies. When he spotted her, he left them and came across.

'Sorry! Every time I give one of these dos, I wonder why I invite so many people, but where do I draw the line? Folk are so easily offended. I haven't even introduced you to my sister.' He glanced round. 'Heaven knows where she's at in this lot.'

'It's not important, Granville. I merely came across to say thanks and to tell you I'm leaving.'

'Don't go! Hang on another hour or so and then it'll thin out.'

She shook her head and insisted, 'By then you'll need peace and quiet. I'll be in touch.'

He shrugged and took her hands in his. 'If you must. Sally will be here till the end of the week. Perhaps we can get together for a meal before she leaves?'

'Perhaps.' Sharon ought to have blocked his intention of introducing her to his sister straight away. He was pulling in the net, and she should be cutting the lines before it got too complicated. But she was too lily-livered to do so on a day like this.

He leaned forward and kissed her cheek again. Extracting her hands from his grip, she smiled. 'Bye!'

'Bye. And thanks for coming.'

She nodded and turned away. He was soon lost in the crowd.

She stood fleetingly on the top step and breathed in the cool air. She'd almost reached her Mini when Craig came alongside.

'Are you going home?'

'Yes.'

'Can you give me a lift to the village?'

'How did you get here?'

'Mildred gave me directions and told me it was a pleasant walk from the village. As it was a nice morning, and I felt like some exercise, I took her advice.' He gave her a sheepish smile. 'Mildred even gave me an old rag to polish my shoes before I actually entered the house. I think she's dying to hear about what it's like inside. I've a feeling she'll question me closely when I get back.'

Sharon couldn't help smiling. 'I expect she will. Most people are curious about what goes on up at the 'big house'.' She decided not to ask why he didn't want to return the same way that he'd come. She turned toward her car. 'Come on, then.' She unlocked it and got in with practised ease. He had more trouble folding his long body into the seat, but she didn't comment and he didn't complain. He even had to bend his head slightly once he was seated because it touched the roof. Clearly, a Mini wasn't intended to comfortably carry someone who was long-limbed and six feet tall.

They set off, and Craig commented positively about the local scenery as he looked out of the window during the short journey. He seemed to like the area. Sharon stopped in front of the pub.

Craig opened the door and unfolded

his form again. 'And what are you planning for the rest of today?'

Her hair bounced around her shoulders and she smiled. 'A quiet evening with a book or the telly.'

'They're having a darts match in the pub. Interested?'

Her brows lifted and her voice was lively. 'I can't throw a dart straight to save my life! They know that. They've given up inviting me.'

'But you're good at other things.' He had his hands on the framework and was bent down. Their eyes met and her pulse quickened. 'Thanks for the lift! I hope that you enjoy your evening with your book. I'm an avid reader too. I'll see you tomorrow?'

'You're welcome. Yes, till tomorrow.'

She revved the engine and glanced in the rear window. He was still standing outside the pub, watching. The pub sign and the strands of loose ivy clinging to the walls were moving in the wind. When she reached the bend in the road, she saw Craig disappear inside. The man was danger with a capital D. She needed to be unconcerned. Trouble was, he was too attractive to ignore. At least he didn't seem to be deliberately trying to attract attention. He had an open friendliness and the kind of presence you couldn't ignore. It was extremely easy to like someone like him.

3

The next day, Sharon didn't see more of him than his raised hand as she was passing through the main office. She lifted hers in return and rippled her fingers.

A customer rang almost before she'd taken her jacket off. Someone was complaining because his urgent order hadn't arrived. One of his regular customers was getting impatient. Sorting that problem took most of the morning. In the end, they found that the order marked 'priority' was at the bottom of a pile of waiting orders.

Sam scratched his head. 'I don't know how that's happened, Miss Vaughan. I always put urgent stuff on top of the pile whenever I get it, so that it gets priority treatment. It's never happened before.' He looked worried. 'John hasn't worked with me very long, but he is very reliable.'

Relieved to find what had gone wrong, she pronounced, 'I know how conscientious you are, Sam. Get it ready and out as an urgent delivery; out before lunch, please.'

Studying the order, Sam nodded. 'There are just a few items. I'll pack them up and get them on the road within the next hour.' Sharon nodded and was about to leave when Sam added, 'Oh! Before you leave. That chap upstairs — he wanted to check the warehouse stock and me to explain what we do. Is that okay?'

She asked, 'He wants to confirm how much we have in store, what's due to leave, that sort of thing?'

Sam shrugged and nodded. 'He wanted to check entries and despatches.'

Sharon wondered why, but there was no reason for her to object. Sam was reliable and a good worker. The finished items were always properly stored and organized. 'Yes, that's okay. I've been told to co-operate fully, so go ahead.'

'I don't dislike him. I've met him in the pub a couple of times and he's okay. He plays darts with the locals, and John was telling me he watches the local football team regularly.'

Sharon nodded. Perhaps mixing in with the locals and gaining their trust was Craig's way of finding out what would otherwise remain hidden to him. 'I'll contact the customer straight away and tell him his stuff will be on its way via special delivery within hours. Give me the details when you have them. I'll email it to him, and he can start tracing where the parcel is instead of bothering us.'

Sam grinned. 'Will do! In future, I'll check through the pile every morning for urgent orders. Perhaps someone messed things up looking for something else and put it back out of order.'

'Perhaps, but there's not much point in worrying about it any more. Just get the order on the road as soon as possible, Sam.'

She looked at Craig's office on the

way back upstairs. The room was blanketed in darkness. In her office, she phoned the customer and told him his order had priority treatment and apologized for the delay. A few minutes later, while getting some coffee, Gaynor mentioned a previous customer of Craig's wanted more details about his report, and it meant he had to go back to head office for a day or two. He wouldn't be back until the end of the week.

Gaynor pulled her sandwich box out of her capacious shoulderbag and fetched a mug of coffee. 'Ready for a break?'

'I shouldn't — I've lost too much time already. I haven't even opened my post yet.'

'Oh come on, it can wait. Grab yourself a chair and your sandwiches, and tell me about Sunday. Was the party a success?'

Sharon gave in and returned with her sandwich box. 'It wasn't a party, it was a reception.'

'Well, whatever you call it. Did you enjoy it?'

Munching away, Sharon replied, 'When you don't know many people, it's not all smiles and sunshine. I'm not very good at small talk. I didn't stay very long. I met the vicar and his family, and Doctor Smallwood and his wife.'

'I don't think I'd feel very happy among that lot; too formal for my liking. I feel sorry for the vicar's daughter. My oldest lad, Mike was in the same class and often told me some others made fun of her because she could never join anything spontaneously. She always needed her mother's approval.'

'I noticed that the mother is rather overbearing. It's not wrong for parents to keep a close eye on their kids, the things that some youngsters get up to these days are hair-raising, but I did get the impression that Gloria wants to do her own thing, but doesn't know how.'

'If she doesn't do something soon,

she'll end up like Minnie Roberts.'

'Who's Minnie Roberts?'

'Never heard of her? She's still working in the offices of the lawyers she joined when she left school thirty-five years ago. Her father died years ago — he was one of the partners in the firm. She wears the same kind of sensible old-fashioned clothes all the time and goes straight home after work. I feel sorry for her. The only time I ever see her is in church on Sunday, provided I go. Her mother is a despotic woman and she's ruining her daughter's chances of leading her own life. Gloria Walters will end up the same as Minnie if she's not careful.'

Sharon nodded. 'Well, I did try to persuade her to rebel a little, and I think Craig did too.'

'Craig? Craig was there?' Gaynor's eyebrows shot halfway up her forehead.

'Yes. I expect Granville invited him because he's a stranger and representing a special firm. I don't think he enjoyed himself much. In fact, I found him hidden away behind the greenery in the conservatory.'

'Then he was bored. He doesn't generally avoid company. He chats to everyone here without any kind of reservation.'

'Then he was just doing his duty, as they say.'

Brushing some crumbs off her skirt, Gaynor changed the subject. 'What about the weekend? Coming to that art exhibition — the one I told you about? Ken suggested we could go for a walk on Hindle's Hill afterwards. He used to go there with his granddad and tells me there's a grand view of the surrounding countryside from the top.'

'Yes, why not. Some fresh air would do me good. I spend too much time indoors on the weekend.'

'So do I; but you have to catch up with shopping, housework, ironing and the rest sometime or other, don't you? You'd never believe the state of the rugby stuff my two bring home every week. I've got to soak it overnight,

67

otherwise I'd never get it clean.'

Sharon joked, 'You spoil them. They should pull their weight. Start training them to do their own washing, before it's too late! Washing is the easy part; the ironing is the tough bit.'

'I try to knock sense into them, but they know I'll give in because I can't stand the sight of that pile of brown mucky shirts on the floor in the outhouse.'

Sharon never expected to find she missed Craig, especially as he hadn't been with them long and she'd had little to do with him. His office was dark and deserted, and she glanced too often at it over the next couple of days.

One afternoon down in the working area, Sandra asked where he was. 'I haven't seen Craig for a couple of days. Is he ill?'

Sharon had to stop telling her to mind her own business. Instead, she managed a composed, 'He needs to take care of some business in Reading. He'll be back.' She picked up a sample design from the table and turned away.

'Oh! I see.' Sandra flicked her shining blond hair off her shoulders and then concentrated on her painting work again.

Walking back to her office, Sharon almost wished Craig had never come to the company. He was ruffling too many feathers. She certainly wasn't interested in him in the way that Sandra was. The trouble was, she couldn't define exactly in what way she was.

Granville phoned. 'What about us meeting this week? Thursday? Sally's leaving on Friday.'

Sharon crossed her fingers and hoped that he wouldn't check her excuses. 'Sorry, Granville; I can't. I've promised to help with posters for the church tower appeal, and I've also already promised to meet someone else after work on Thursday.'

He paused. 'Pity! Still there's bound to be another chance, soon I hope.'

Sharon remained silent.

'I'll phone again on the weekend or

at the beginning of next week. We must meet soon. Bye!'

'Bye! Thanks for the invitation, and greetings to your sister.' Sharon hadn't yet plucked up enough courage to be honest and tell him there was no reason for her to meet his sister. She had to explain how she felt first — face to face.

* * *

Friday morning Craig returned. Even though she didn't know what they were talking about, she could tell Gaynor was fencing with him indulgently. She heard him chuckling. She felt a warm glow and had to stop herself rushing out to say hello.

She was glad she had a genuine reason to be there when she handed Gaynor some work, and looked across to see Craig standing in his doorway. Her smile came easily. He seemed pleased with himself too. 'Hi there!' he said. One large hand gripped the wooden framework and the other was stuck in his trouser pocket.

'Hi. Back from the big city, I see.'

He grinned. 'The city in question wasn't that big.'

'Well, it's a lot bigger than this place.'

'True, but not nicer.'

She nodded. When he looked at her, she suddenly felt a gamut of perplexing emotions. She looked away quickly. 'I'll agree with you there. People down south underestimate the attractions of the Midlands.'

His mouth turned up at the corners as he eyed her carefully. 'You can say that again. Gaynor just told me you're coming to the exhibition on Sunday.'

Looking puzzled, she uttered, 'Yes. Are you?'

He nodded. 'She invited me, and I'm looking forward to it very much.' His smoky eyes held her gaze.

She wished she didn't feel a surge of excitement; such a silly reaction. She rallied quickly and commented, 'Me too.'

The sound of her telephone saved the day. She was almost grateful to turn away without further ado and order her thoughts. She wondered briefly if she'd have agreed, knowing Gaynor intended to invite him too. Probably not. Gaynor was like that; she was a kindly soul with a heart of gold. Sharon busied herself with checking some contracts and was glad that it demanded all her concentration.

Gaynor popped her head round the door just before she left. Sharon made a quiet hissing sound, pointed in the direction of the cubbyhole and then beckoned her in. 'Stop acting like the spy who came in from the cold,' Gaynor said. 'He's gone.'

'Why didn't you tell me you'd invited him?'

'Because when I asked you, I hadn't. We were talking after he got back, and he asked what people could do on the weekends around here. I suddenly realized it must be boring for him. He hasn't got a family or friends nearby. It seemed natural to ask him along. Why? Do you object?'

'No, I just wondered why.' She paused. 'I hope you're not trying to pair me off again, because I'm not having it. Confine your matchmaking to someone like Gloria or Minnie! I'm quite capable of finding my own boyfriends.' Sharon was recalling Gaynor's attempts to match her up with a sales representative. She still cringed with embarrassment when she recalled how she had to explain to him that Gaynor had misunderstood the situation and wanted to push them together. He'd avoided coming to the company ever since, and always sent a substitute.

'Well, look what happens when you're left to your own devices! You end up with someone like Granville! I'm not being devious, cross my heart. I just thought he'd enjoy it. He's a pleasant chap.'

'What time on Sunday?'

'We'll pick you up about one-thirty. It's on our way. Craig will meet us outside the gallery at two. He's going to watch the locals playing in an away game first.'

* * *

Autumn was in the air, and grey clouds were racing across the sky far above them. Sharon was in the back of the car, listening to the banter between Gaynor and Ken. Even though they had two grown-up sons, they were completely involved in each other. In Sharon's eyes, they were a happy pair. They had a good sense of fun and shared everything. Ken was the quieter of the two but they understood each other blind. She enjoyed being with them. She thought about how her cousin and his wife bickered constantly whenever she saw them these days. Her mother had pooh-poohed the idea when Sharon mentioned she thought they might be breaking up.

Ken chose a zigzag route along narrow roads, over humpback bridges, and through various villages and farmland. The cool temperatures weren't putting people off sitting outside pubs with a drink or a meal in the fresh air. Sharon liked the surrounding countryside. The nearby rural scenery had played a part in her decision to buy her cottage. She couldn't imagine living in a large town with all its anonymity anymore, even though she'd gone to university in Leicester and enjoyed her time there too.

Craig was waiting when they arrived. The match had finished early. Sharon viewed him with studied detachment. She smiled at him, and he smiled back.

The exhibition was in a Victorian building and there was no entrance fee. They wandered the rooms and looked at works by professionals and amateurs. There was a very impressive selection of paintings by local art students in one room, and several of them were breathtaking. When he realized that paintings by amateurs were also on display, Ken's imagination was fired.

Craig commented, 'I don't know how good you are, but why don't you get in touch with the organizers and find out about the conditions of entry?'

Two hours later, they all agreed it had been enjoyable, and now it was time for some fresh air. They were soon strolling up a hill towards groups of scattered bushes and grey rocks that stood defiantly just below the summit. Underfoot the grass was hard and dry, and gorse grew between jagged protruding boulders. The footworn pathway was narrow in places and they had to walk in single file. Sharon didn't mind, as it gave her time to ponder. The warm weather was over for this year, and with the wind whistling and no one else in sight, the place seemed almost wild and inhospitable. The footpath, or what was left of it, wound lazily along until they reached the outcrop of rocks that glinted grey and shiny in the midday sun. From there, the path forked off in two directions.

Gaynor looked at her watch. 'Do we

have time to go further?'

Sharon looked back. In summer, this place was doubtless an attractive spot. 'I don't mind what we do, but this isn't a bad spot to take a break. The rocks give us some shelter from the wind.' She looked up. 'Clouds are gathering, and we may have to dash back.'

Ken nodded in agreement. 'You're right. I'd like to take some photos before we leave. Won't be long. It's a lovely view from here, isn't it?'

Craig answered, 'Just great. We're lucky that the rain has held off, otherwise we wouldn't see much.'

Gaynor didn't stay with them. She went off with Ken. Sharon watched them gesturing and moving from place to place as Ken took some photos. Sharon sat in a shallow cavity in the largest rock. Craig joined her. She was very aware of his nearness. He leaned forward and his glance drifted across the landscape. The wind ruffled his hair and he looked tough, lean and athletic. Cut off from the direct wind, the sun was warm on her face. She felt a surge of pleasure and knew she could easily lose herself in being with this man. She needed to control her thoughts and ignore the temptation of engaging him in too much private conversation; that would show him she was interested. She didn't need a meaningless affair, and Craig was just passing through. She fumbled in her mind for a sensible remark. 'Sam mentioned you asked about the stores and the storeroom. Why?'

Was it just her imagination, or did the animation leave his face to be replaced by a look of disappointment before he straightened? 'Now and then I do a spot check and match the records.'

'And?' Sharon felt stronger now that they were talking business.

'I'm afraid the production and despatch figures don't.'

Startled, she uttered, 'What do you mean?'

He bent one knee and stuck the other

leg out in a straight line. 'Just that. They don't match. The production figures don't match with what Sam's despatched, plus what's still on the shelves.'

She blurted out hurriedly, 'You mean there should be more in stock than there is?'

'Yes. I didn't want to bring it up today.' He shrugged. 'Still, since you started this conversation, I may as well go on. I think over the period of several months about thirty sets of coffee or dinner services have disappeared. Perhaps I've miscalculated something, and I do intend to check again. It's not my job to look for theft or point it out, but I've made an exception because in this case the loss will make a big difference to your annual profit. I simply intended to take a quick look and compare. Normally I take statistics at face value, but some instinct told me something was wrong.'

Sharon was lost for words and chewed her lip. 'Thirty sets? That's a lot of money. Are you sure?'

He shook his head. 'Not absolutely. Like I said, I'll check again; and assuming I'm right, you'll have to find out exactly what's happening before you take official steps. Who has access to the production and the stores accounts?'

'The head of the sections should be the only one who knows the password, but I presume others working there know it too. In other words, Sam is responsible for despatch and Ken for production.'

He rubbed his chin. 'Well, there's something funny going on somewhere. Don't mention it to anyone yet. I hope you don't mind my unintentional interference?' Seeing her expression, he tried to lessen her surprise with a smile. 'Don't start to worry yet. Perhaps it's all my imagination. Let's enjoy what's left of the afternoon.' He reached out and took her hand in his. She noted that even the feel of his hand had the power to stir her in a way she'd never experienced before. She was too surprised to do anything but nod. She withdrew her hand and pretended to brush the hair off her face. Their eyes met and she felt a shock run through her.

She managed to sound unconcerned. 'I can't pretend I'm not worried. I hope you find you were mistaken.' She cleared her throat and tried to control the racing currents in her brain. Was it the news about the company, or the effect of him holding her hand?

His expression grew serious, and Sharon was almost glad to see Gaynor and Ken returning. She got up quickly and brushed the seat of her pants and shoved her hands into her pockets. Craig was quiet and withdrawn, and she didn't try to break the silence. They stood stiffly side by side, watching the other two coming towards them.

The afternoon sun had faded and the wind was blowing in their faces. Sharon looked at her watch and was surprised to see how quickly the time had passed.

From here, the route down to the floor of the valley was straightforward. They followed each other and, by the time they'd reached their cars, daylight was fading.

Gaynor asked, 'As you'll be going back to the pub, Craig, will you take Sharon with you and drop her off on the way? Then we can take the back road and be home quicker.'

'No problem.' He was busy unlocking the door. Sharon couldn't see his face. She genuinely hoped he didn't mind. He declared, 'I'll be glad to have someone with me who knows the way. I haven't a clue where we are. Thanks for the invitation. I really enjoyed myself.'

Gaynor beamed. 'Did you? That's good. You must come round for supper one evening.'

'Love to.' He opened the door on the passenger side and left it ajar before he got into the driving seat. Sharon echoed his thanks and joined him. Searching for something bright to say, she commented, 'At least you don't have to fold yourself into this car.'

Concentrating on leaving the car park, he replied, 'No, it's reliable and comfortable. I can find my way back to the town, but I'll be lost after that. It'll save me bothering with the GPS.'

'Sure. Main roads or the countrified alternative?'

His voice was curt. 'I don't mind, as long as you give me the directions early enough.'

Sharon's heart sank. He looked as if he was annoyed. He ran his hand down his face, put the radio on, and some pop music played quietly in the background. It filled the awkwardness she felt. He was soon pulling up outside her cottage. He looked with interest at the ivy that criss-crossed the reddish brickwork, and the old apple tree defying the elements in the tiny front garden, then looked ahead again quickly without comment. Sharon wondered if he was hoping she'd invite him in. She was too confused about him and didn't want to complicate her life. He was just like a drifting leaf in autumn — here today, gone tomorrow. She couldn't afford to give him any encouragement.

He didn't release his safety belt. Sharon scrambled out quickly. She slammed the door and raised her hand in thanks. He acknowledged with a cursory dip of his head without looking at her, and drove off. Sharon almost wished that she could explain why she wanted to keep her distance. She enjoyed being with him, but he might be used to passing affairs with willing females wherever he happened to be. She didn't want to be just another one of those women. A tumble of confused thoughts and feelings washed over her as she scrabbled in her bag looking for her key. She told herself to ignore him.

Inside her own home, familiar surroundings had a stabilizing effect on her thoughts. She concentrated on getting herself an evening meal and told herself to focus on running the firm. Craig

Baines wasn't half as important as the pottery. She almost convinced herself of that before she went to bed.

4

The coffee machine was bubbling away when Sharon arrived at work on Monday morning, and she was almost glad to see that Craig's office was empty. She set to work and hurried to get waiting tasks out of the way so that she could check for the discrepancies he'd found. She was interrupted when Granville phoned.

'Let's meet,' he said. 'I've a parish meeting this evening, so what about tomorrow?'

Sharon decided this was her chance to tell him how she felt. 'Yes, that's fine. Where?'

'The Fox and Hounds? Seven?'

'Right.'

'Good. Looking forward to seeing you again.'

She bit her tongue. 'Anyone would think we hadn't seen each other for months. See you tomorrow.'

Ending their call, she wondered when they met whether to tell him point blank, or to be more tactful. She pushed that problem aside and picked up the letter in front on her on the desk. First things first!

By lunchtime, she had cleared most of her timetable for the day. She still wasn't convinced that Craig had found anything amiss, but had to admit that he knew enough about company structures and accounting to spot an irregularity. She loaded some of the relevant accounts on her computer screen. Her colour heightened slightly when a knock on the door made her look up and she saw Craig.

He hovered in the doorway. His features were blank. 'Hi! Finished your lunch?'

She hoped she sounded nonchalant. 'Yes.'

'Good. I'd like to show you what I mentioned yesterday. It won't take long.'

'Actually, I was just about to take a look myself.'

He nodded, grabbed a chair, and sat down next to her. There was a fascinating air of efficiency about him, and she was conscious of his virile appeal. Sharon took a deep breath and concentrated on the monitor.

Sitting alongside, one arm draped along the back of her chair, he looked at the computer. 'Good! It's easiest to spot if you take production figures and deduct the warehouse's dispatches. That should match what's on the shelves, but it doesn't. Even when you take unsold items from past months and possible breakages in the despatching process into account, there's still a disparity.' He leaned forward and it sent a dizzying current through her being. 'The figures just don't balance.'

Sharon concentrated hard and calculated. She managed to nod, and a frown covered her face. 'Yes, something is wrong. Why didn't I notice it?'

He shrugged. 'Unless you make a

detailed comparison of the whole month, you wouldn't. You might miss it even then. As long as everything balances, no one is inclined to check every entry with a magnifying glass.'

'Could it be a computer hiccup?'

He tilted his head and declared cynically, 'Do you honestly believe computing errors would be between production and dispatch, and nowhere else in the system? I haven't found any others.'

Sharon leaned back. 'I'm stunned. I know all the workers. I interviewed every single one of them. It isn't just an occasional cup and saucer, is it?'

He shook his head. 'According to my calculations, we're talking about complete sets.'

'I wonder how long it's been going on. I can't believe anyone here would be so devious.'

Craig's grey eyes narrowed. 'My curiosity was wakened when I noticed someone was adjusting monthly statistics using the same phrase. People usually vary their formulation, often out of sheer boredom. Production and the warehouse start off with the same amount. All well and good, I thought. Then I noticed that the warehouse stock was being reduced regularly, using the phrase 'sub-standard item'. As production pre-sorts sub-standard items out before they finish their calculations, I wondered what was going on. The deduction used the same formulation every time, and that heightened my interest. I added these 'sub-standard' items together for one month and found it exactly matched an amount reduced from the production data for that month. It was labelled 'cost reduction' — but normally that has nothing to do with production. You decide on whether to work with cost reduction before production runs. As the various sections have no reason to constantly back-check their entries for the current or previous months, as long as they balanced no one noticed, and the altered balances were carried forward to the following month.'

Angry, Sharon blurted, 'But that means someone unauthorized has the computer passwords for the production and the warehouse! Only Gaynor and I know them all.'

His eyes were contemplative and he tried to be supportive. He shrugged. 'Someone's being very clever.'

'I'd put my hand in the fire for Gaynor. I'm sure she's not involved.'

'I don't know her well, but I agree. Generally people with sticky fingers are a certain kind of character. Gaynor is too practical and contented with her lot.'

Sharon felt his arm along her shoulder and wanted to pull back, but knew he'd notice and wonder why. She blinked hard, and there was a tingling in the pit of her stomach. She met his glance again as casually as she could manage and nodded in silent agreement. 'It will make a big difference. Complete services are expensive. If you're right, and a decent number have been stolen, we're talking about real money.'

'Yes. You're a small company, and your firing costs alone are astronomical. You can't afford any kind of thieving. Someone's pinching your profits.'

She brushed her hair off her face, leaned forward and stared at the statistics on the screen. 'I can't and don't believe Sam is responsible. Who else, though? John hasn't been with us long, but Sam says he's trying hard. I wonder if it could be Ken, or someone else from his section. Do I go to the police? What do you suggest we do?'

'It's not up to me, but I'd try to get proof first. I'd install a camera. Video systems are very sophisticated these days. They function wirelessly. You'd need to hide the recorder somewhere and check it daily till you find the culprit.'

Sharon masked her nervousness with deceptive calm as her brain ticked over. 'A camera covering Sam's desk and the packing area from a high shelf would be easier than trying to cover the production area. I don't think Sam would notice anything for a while, because older or less popular items are stored on the top shelves.' She paused and bit her lip. 'But as soon as I employ a firm to fix a camera, word will soon spread and it'll be counterproductive.'

Craig was quiet for a moment. 'If you like, I'll find out what you need and how to install it, then do the job on Sunday when the factory is deserted. But you shouldn't tell anyone what you're doing, not even Gaynor! Everyone is a possible suspect.'

'Yes, I see what you mean. If you sort out the camera side of things, it'll save me a lot of hassle. Generally the factory is deserted on the weekend unless there's a special order.'

He stood up. 'Good. I'll let you know as soon as I've found what we need.'

She looked at him and tried to throttle the dizzying current racing through her. She looked down and hoped he hadn't seen the longing in her expression. In control again, she exclaimed, 'Thanks! Especially as this isn't part of your job, is it?'

He confessed, 'No, definitely not. I'm here to gather statistics, work with formulas, make observations and offer suggestions.'

'It sounds very clinical.'

'Does it? You'd be surprised how you can make good forecasts with the right information and formulas.'

'You seem to like your job.'

'I wanted one that requires mathematical skills. Numbers have always fascinated me. One day, when I get fed up with moving around, perhaps I'll start my own company doing the same thing. It doesn't matter what the end product is; the same rules apply to everything.' He viewed her indulgently. 'You do your work instinctively; I do mine using formulas and logic.'

She tilted her head to the side and smiled. 'I studied business management. I also consider the pros and cons when I make a decision.'

'Ah, but you allow human reasoning to influence your decisions. I don't. I just follow rules! No emotion involved, just figures and decimals.' He got up, gave her a last lingering look before he put the chair back, and went out.

Sharon tried to ignore the knowledge that someone was thieving. She got on with her work and eventually managed to push it to the back of her mind for a while.

* * *

She felt nervous the next evening when she was getting ready to meet Granville, and worried about how he'd react. She was early, but he was already waiting in the corner of the elegant dining room. There weren't many other guests. Granville had been studying the menu. He put it down and got up when she came towards him.

He pulled out her chair and she sat down. 'That's good; you're early. That's one of the things I like about you.

You're always punctual.'

Sharon shoved her bag under the table and gave him a friendly smile. 'Thank my mother! She always insisted we were punctual, no matter what we were doing. I grew up thinking lateness was a crime.'

'I hope to meet her one day soon.' He handed her his menu. 'I'm going to have the fish. What would you like? Do you want a starter?'

She shook her head and was careful not let their fingers touch. 'No, thanks.' She looked around. 'This is a nice place, isn't it? I know that we came here once before, weeks and weeks ago, but that was for lunch. Places always look different when the lights are low.'

While she studied the menu, he talked about the history of the place. Sharon listened with half an ear. She had no real appetite, and wondered how to start to tell Granville the real reason why she'd come. She didn't want to hurt him; but on the assumption he was thinking along more permanent lines, she couldn't let him go on doing so. 'I'll have the steak with a baked potato and beans.' She closed the menu and looked up again. She had another moment's reprise as the waitress took their order and Granville ordered them some wine.

When the waitress disappeared, Granville noticed Sharon's anxious expression. 'Anything wrong? You look tense. Something amiss at the factory?'

'No, it's nothing to do with work.' The theft at the factory must wait for another time. She was silent for only for a moment. She realized she had to be honest with him. 'I need to talk about something that bothers me, and hope you'll understand.'

'Something serious? What's the matter?'

'I think you and I see our friendship in two very differing ways.' She cleared her throat. 'Recently people have told me that our names are linked seriously. I've always considered us to be good friends, but not more than that.'

Granville reached out across the table to take her hand. Sharon didn't withdraw it. She ploughed on. 'You're a nice man, Granville. I really like you. But I'm not in love with you.'

His blue eyes were suddenly troubled. He hurried to interrupt. 'I haven't told you so before now because I was waiting for the right moment, but I am in love with you, Sharon.'

She swallowed hard and met his glance. 'You're one of the nicest men I know, but that's not enough.'

Trying to smother her words, he uttered, 'Give us more time. I think you'll come round when we see each other more often. We get on well. You're clever and beautiful and a caring person. Just the kind of woman I want at my side.'

She paused and looked down at their joined hands. 'No; it wouldn't work, Granville. I'm flattered that you could even consider me in that way, but I wouldn't be happy living in your world. I'm not interested in social gatherings, horse riding, horse racing, polo, golf, holidays in the south of France, or shooting forays in Scotland in the autumn. I could never warm to that kind of life. You must have noticed that.'

'My friends like you and you'll get used to them. Don't push me aside because of that.'

She noticed he didn't suggest he'd compromise to suit her philosophy. Why on earth did he believe it could work? She shook her head. 'I'm not pushing you aside. I just don't want more than friendship.'

His expression stiffened and his eyes grew colder. 'That's not enough for me. I want more than mere friendship. I presumed you felt the same. It seems I've completely misjudged the situation. I suppose I must be grateful that you've been honest with me.'

Sharon withdrew her hand and he didn't try to hang on. 'I'm sorry if you got the wrong impression. I had no intention of leading you on, as the expression goes.'

He said between thinned lips, 'Is there someone else?'

'No.'

'Then I don't see why we just can't carry on as we're doing now.'

'Because it wouldn't work! It wouldn't lead anywhere. Friendship is one thing; love is something else. Knowing we feel differently means we'll have difficulty holding even an ordinary conversation. I won't change my mind, and we can't pretend now that we never talked about how we stand.'

He studied her, laid his serviette to one side, and got up. His expression was stony, 'In other words, you're giving me the brush-off? Then if you'll excuse me, I'll settle the bill on the way out!' Without looking back, he left hurriedly.

Sharon was glued to the spot for a moment, but she was also relieved that she'd been truthful even though Granville might feel upset and let down. Crumpling her own serviette, she got up. She hurried to retrieve her coat and, with a nod to the startled waitress, she went outside.

She saw the red tail-lights of Granville's car in the distance, and hoped he wouldn't hate her too much for being honest. She'd never knowingly misled him. If other people hadn't made her aware of the gossip, she would have carried on seeing him occasionally. That would have raised his expectations even more. On the way back to her cottage, she hoped their business relationship would remain cordial. She didn't move in the same kind of social circles as he did, so she wouldn't see him often outside work. He had to come to the factory to attend board meetings. They were both sensible and ought to be able to cope in a civilized way.

She viewed the narrow roadway disappearing behind her in the rear mirror, and wished life was more straightforward. Even good relationships sometimes had their limitations when people forgot to be completely honest with each other.

5

Sharon thought about phoning Granville the next day. She wanted to clear the air between them, but ultimately decided she'd wait until things had calmed of their own accord.

Gaynor persuaded her to come to the Halloween costume party at the pub. Anyone and everyone was invited. There was no point in staying at home every day. She'd cleared the position with Granville and she should get out more.

When Sharon arrived, the small tables were decorated with orange dahlias, and most of them were already occupied. A large numbers of yellow and carrot-coloured pumpkins had been strategically placed. The main lighting had been dimmed, and some of the pumpkins had been hollowed out and had a lighted candle inside.

Cut-outs of small jet-black vampires undulated on strings from the ceiling. The corners and niches were draped in black and painted with skeletons and bizarre-looking faces. The windows had been painted black too, and lots of fat candles of various heights burned brightly on the windowsills. Sharon wondered briefly how long it had taken to decorate the room; it looked great.

She hadn't spent as much time on her costume as most of the others present. Some villagers had elaborate ones, including cloaks, made-up faces, and complicated coloured hairstyles. Some hadn't made much effort, and others turned up in what they always wore. One of the regulars had his leg pulled by one and all when they announced he had the best Halloween costume of the evening, even though he turned up in the same baggy pants and shapeless pullover he always wore. He took it in good stead.

Sharon had chosen black jeans, a black hoody over an old black T-shirt sporting a white skeleton, and black boots. She'd plastered on black eye makeup, covered her skin in talcum powder, left her lips bare, and sprayed her hair to stand on end. Ken and Gaynor were in one of the corners and she squeezed through the throng to join them. A lot of people present were workers in the factory. She exchanged a word here and there and finally reached them. She eyed Ken as Dracula, and Gaynor as a witch, complete with pointed hat and hooked nose. 'Where did you get that nose?' she laughed. 'It's awful!'

Gaynor smiled. 'I'm glad you don't think it's mine! I bought it, of course, and let my hair dry of its own accord — that's why I look like I've been dragged through a hedge backwards. Ken borrowed his costume from one of the boys. I just did his face and added the streaks of blood.'

Ken grimaced and piped in, 'I feel a right Charlie, I can tell you!'

Sharon scrutinized him and chuckled. 'Well, you look great.'

Ken got up and picked up their empty glasses. 'What can I get you?'

'A lager, please. And the next round is on me.'

Ken went off to the bar. Gaynor chatted about the costumes. The noise increased by the minute. She suddenly noticed Craig was coming towards them.

'Oh, look! Craig,' Gaynor said. 'I thought he might not bother. Doesn't he look super? Someone must've given him gel for his hair. He looks quite dodgy.'

Sharon was too busy experiencing various emotions to reply. Disconcerted, she left the initial greetings to Gaynor.

His eyes swept over them. 'Everyone's in the spirit of the thing, I see. Don't cast any nasty spells on me, Gaynor!'

'As long as you behave yourself, you're safe.'

He nodded and looked Sharon. 'I didn't expect to see you here this evening.'

She breathed in deeply and wished he didn't bewilder her so easily. He'd be gone soon again. 'A spontaneous decision.' She gestured. 'I'm glad I've come, though. Everyone's made an effort, including you.'

He shrugged. 'Mildred plastered this stuff on my hair. I expect I'll have to shower for ages to get the damned stuff off afterwards, but I suspect plenty of other people will need lots of energetic scrubbing in the shower to look normal tomorrow.'

Sharon didn't want to imagine Craig in the shower. The idea made her dizzy. 'Yes. As well as a daddy of a headache too by the time the pub closes tonight.'

He glanced around. 'Mildred and her husband have put a lot of work into it.'

Feeling she had to converse, she answered, 'Yes, they're always thinking up something special. It's good for business, and it's also good for the community of course.'

He nodded, and to her consternation he squeezed in next to her. His nearness made her feel like a breathless girl of eighteen who'd just managed to attract the attention of the most popular upper-form heart-throb. She wanted to deny the effect he was having on her but didn't know how.

When Ken returned, he offered to get Craig a drink.

'Don't bother. I've promised people over there in the corner to have a drink with them, but I'll be back later.' He disappeared into the crowd again.

Gaynor remarked, 'It's surprising how well he's assimilated into the local scene, isn't it? Most people know he's come to do an unpopular job, but they still like him.'

Sharon eyed his tall figure as he fought his way to the other side of the room, and continued to watch him from afar. She mentally shook herself. 'He told me he's used to facing initial opposition everywhere he goes, but he's learned to live with it. He's essentially a person who just adjusts to his sur-roundings and the situation as best he can. Basically he's okay; even I admit that. He fits in easily because he's not stand-offish.'

Sharon had to stop making too many positive remarks about him. She surveyed him surreptitiously as he chatted to some people. One of them was Sandra, who was hanging on the arm of someone with reddish hair and blue eyes. Sharon told herself she was just impressionable because she'd met him when she'd had the courage to break with Granville, and he dazed her because of the way he worked and won people over.

The noise and the fun continued. Mildred had organized a quiz; the questions had to do with Halloween. Some of the answers were just as weird as the questions. She'd also organized 'dipping the apples', and put the names of everyone present into a hat. She drew out six, and Sharon's was one of them. There was a cheer from the workers from the factory and comments about 'flying the flag', and

108

'showing 'em what's what'.

She flushed but stood up and joined the other five standing around a plastic bucket on a chair. Sharon remembered playing it as a child; it had been fun in those days. Now she prayed she wouldn't make a fool of herself. Someone was timing their efforts. Sharon was third. The first two didn't do very well, although in the end one of them did manage to bite into one of the apples. The set limit was four minutes.

Sharon bent down and put her hands behind her back. The chap with the stopwatch said 'Go!' and Sharon pushed an apple towards the rim with her chin and then concentrated on getting her teeth into it. Her face was soon soaking, but she pulled it out of the water.

'One minute twenty seconds!'

She grinned when she heard the cheers. She lost her balance and toppled into Craig's arms. Quickly she disengaged and grabbed the towel he was holding. It soon absorbed most of her eye makeup and left her face full of black streaks.

He burst out laughing. 'Well done!'

She felt the heat from his body, and his breath was in her hair. With heightened colour, she froze as she met his glance. 'Thanks.'

'You're welcome.' He winked and tipped his head towards the remaining competitors. 'Let's see if they can do better.'

In the end, she won. Her prize was a bag of apples; and after the clapping and presentation, she went back to Gaynor and Ken. On the way, she passed Sandra and nodded. The man at Sandra's side smiled at her. 'Bravo.'

He was a stranger, but a friendly one. 'Thanks!' she replied.

He explained, 'I'm Raymond Keyes. I joined your accountants Williams and Francis back in March. I don't think we've met, have we?'

Sharon smiled. He was an attractive man and knew how to dress. This evening the Victorian gentleman's costume omitted nothing. He wore a frock coat and charcoal trousers, a wing-collared shirt, a black necktie, and a black waistcoat, and looked like someone straight out of a history book. He was very polite and pleasant too, because he declared, 'I hope we'll meet again soon.'

'Perhaps. I don't have much direct contact with our accountants. Gillian Forster comes in part-time to keep everything up to date. She's a qualified bookkeeper.'

He nodded. 'These days computers save a lot of drudgery, but someone still has to check and balance.'

Trying to be polite, Sharon asked, 'Have you moved locally, or were you already living here when you joined Williams and Francis?'

'I moved here as soon as I found somewhere suitable. I used to live and work in Manchester.'

'Do you like it here?'

He nodded. 'Very much. I've met some nice people, including my partner this evening. You know Sandra of course. She works at the factory.'

Looking irritated, Sandra looked at him and replied, 'Yes. Sometimes I think I've been there too long.'

Sharon was surprised. She was one of their most talented painters. She'd have a chat with her soon and find out what was wrong.

Raymond asked, 'Staying for the fireworks?'

'Are there fireworks? I didn't know that there'd be any. Are fireworks part of Halloween?

He smiled broadly. 'These days anything goes.'

'Yes, you're right. Well, I'd better get back to my friends.'

'Pleased to meet you! See you later I hope?'

Sharon responded with a smile. 'I expect so.

There was lots of singing and general enjoyment as the evening continued. There were also the inevitable skirmishes among some of the younger people who'd drunk too much too fast. Mildred had organized appropriate music for the evening, including 'Whis-tlin' Past the Graveyard', 'Night of the Phantom', and 'Ghostbusters'. At midnight, she announced the fireworks display. They grabbed their coats and streamed out into the yard behind the pub. Two men from a professional company were responsible for the pyrotechnics.

The ground felt damp underfoot. Sharon was glad she was wearing warm boots. Pitch-torches lined the area. Sharon found herself near the front. The atmosphere and the excited voices reminded her of her childhood and Bonfire Night. There was no bonfire tonight, no crackle of burning wood or pungent smell of smoke; but once the display began, she was spellbound by the blossoming stars in all colours of the rainbow. Some exploded outward, while others scattered long tails before they erupted with bangs and flashes of light. Hummers whizzed and crackled in the air, and whistles echoed through the night as blue smoke spread across the field. There was something magical about fireworks.

Sharon pulled up the collar of her coat and enjoyed the moment. She looked around and noticed that Craig was standing with Sandra and Raymond Keyes. He met her glance and winked at her broadly. Briefly she even thought about going across to join them. She couldn't see Ken and Gaynor. While she was still pondering whether to go or not, his attention returned to the display again, so she stayed where she was. One of the men from the factory and his wife started chatting to her while they watched the bursts of colour in the sky.

There were sounds of laughter when people finally left. Everyone agreed they'd enjoyed a grand display and a good evening. Sharon walked part of the way home with Gaynor and Ken. The majority of people were villagers, and those who lived further afield were sensible on the whole and shared taxis to go home. The air was cold and crisp, and there was a silver-edged moon in the sky. Stars twinkled like diamonds above them as their footsteps echoed into the darkness.

Sharon had enjoyed herself, and she thought briefly that Granville wouldn't have done. He preferred more refined, controlled gatherings, and he often had difficulties adjusting to strangers, although he was good at small talk. She parted company from Ken and Gaynor and walked home through the darkness. Fitting her key in the lock, she mused that Craig seemed to feel at ease with people from all kinds of backgrounds. She went inside and locked the door before she headed straight for the narrow staircase. Minutes later, staring at her reflection in the bathroom mirror, she uttered loudly, 'Blast it!' Why did she think about Craig so much? He meant nothing to her.

6

Monday morning, when things got into swing, Sharon dealt with a mixture of acclaim and criticism from customers who seemed to have used the weekend to decide whether to place new orders or not. At lunchtime Craig knocked on the door and came in. He looked back briefly to make sure Gaynor wasn't at her desk. 'Hi! Enjoy the Halloween do?'

She looked up, felt a warm glow, and pushed her hair out of the way. 'Yes. Did you?'

'Absolutely. What did you do with the apples? I must say you gave a very good performance. I bet you'll take a snorkel with you next time!'

'That would be cheating! I left them for Mildred to use. I couldn't have eaten more than a handful before they went bad.'

His eyes twinkled. 'I wanted to check

that you still want me to sort out the video camera. Is that still all right?'

'Yes, of course. I still can't believe it's happened, but figures don't lie, do they? Do you want some money?'

He shook his head and stuck his hands in the pocket of his beige chinos. He looked relaxed and well groomed. His clothes were clearly expensive and classy, but he wore them without ostentatiousness. 'No, that's okay. We can settle the paperwork later. I'll find out if we can hire instead of buying. Some companies will hire out. It sometimes depends on the reason you need the camera. I presume you don't want one on the premises permanently — you just want to find out who's stealing stuff now?'

She fiddled with a pencil, then looked directly into his eyes and nodded. She was glad she was sitting down, and wished her pulse rate didn't accelerate when he was near. 'That'll be great. I don't even know if we're in contradiction of labour laws.'

His expression was thoughtful. 'I think you're okay under the circumstances, but I'll see what I can find. Is the weekend free in the factory? As soon as I get what you need, I could set it up. The sooner, the better.'

'There's nothing special planned this weekend. Is Sunday still good for you?'

He nodded. 'It shouldn't take long to set up.'

* * *

She drove to the pottery after a leisurely breakfast on Sunday, and parked in the yard. Craig was waiting. She got out quickly and her colour heightened as she walked towards him. He was sheltering from the cold wind in one of the doorways. Fumbling for her keys in her bag, she looked up. 'I hope you haven't been waiting long? We did agree on ten o'clock, didn't we?'

He smiled lazily. 'It's five to ten; you're dead on time. I decided to walk in case one of the workers noticed my car nearby and started wondering. I only just got here.'

She noticed the bulging briefcase in his hand. 'And you have all you need?'

He nodded. 'I hired the camera on a weekly basis. The contract automatically extends week after week until it's returned. We might be lucky and catch someone quickly, or nothing might happen for weeks or even months. The chap gave me pretty good terms and explained how to install it.'

Sharon unlocked the door, and once they were inside she followed him through the empty building. Their footsteps echoed and she noticed the building was colder than usual. The heating was automatically reduced on the weekend. All the sections were deserted, and it seemed strange not to hear the noise and constant bustle everywhere. Sharon hadn't been to work very often on a Sunday. She didn't want get into the habit, though once or twice she'd had no alternative.

Craig headed directly to the warehousing section. He took off his overcoat and threw it over Sam's swivel chair by the desk. He was wearing black stretch jeans and a dark polo-neck cable-knit jumper, and looked coolly elegant and in command. He wandered along the shelves looking for the right spot, pointed above where he stood, at a spot that would register any movement near Sam's computer. Sharon nodded her agreement. With quiet assurance, he explained, 'We can't cover the whole room, but they'll have to pass the desk when they come in, and they need to use the computer to adjust the figures. Of course, that's on the assumption they're doing it immediately after stealing something.'

Sharon nodded. 'Be careful! If you fall down and break your neck, it'll be very difficult for me to explain what we were both doing here on a Sunday morning.' He grinned, and Sharon swallowed a lump in her throat.

'You can always tell them we had a

romantic rendezvous.' He chuckled as he studied her face. 'Don't worry; I'll be careful. I know what I'm doing. I'll fix the camera there, but we may have to adjust the angle when we check the picture on the screen in your office.' He positioned a sliding ladder, and once he was at the top he called down, 'Can you get a cloth or a duster? The surface up here is pretty grimy, and I can't tape anything into position unless it's dirt-free.'

Sharon eventually found an old rag and soaked it in the washroom. She climbed the first couple of rungs and Craig leaned down to take it. They were close enough to make her think it was the perfect moment to kiss. She paused for a second while their eyes met. Then he took the cloth and straightened up.

Sharon went back to the desk feeling confused. She reminded herself they were here to do a job. Minutes later, Craig jumped down from the last couple of rungs. He brushed his hands free of dust and gestured her towards the stairway to the offices. Picking up his briefcase, he uttered over his shoulder, 'We need a power socket. Is there somewhere suitable in your office?'

'There are some sockets under the desk. We can put the recorder in the bottom drawer.'

'Sounds just the place. Let's go.'

A short time later, the recorder was connected, but Craig had to return to adjust the camera's position as they found the angle was wrong. Their voices echoed through the rooms as they shouted instructions and agreement. Finally satisfied, Craig came back and demonstrated the recorder's functions. Now Sharon had to check it every morning, and restart it before she left every evening. He washed his hands, and they switched the recorder on before she followed him out.

'Thanks, Craig. I'm very grateful, especially because this is nothing to do with your actual work here.'

He stuck his hands in his pockets.

'How about repaying me by having lunch with me? Or have you something else lined up?'

The breath caught in her lungs. She was too surprised to do more than nod. 'I'd like that. I've nothing special planned.'

'Good! There's a nice little restaurant in Wolversthorpe. I've been there before, but I'll enjoy it more in your company.'

'I know the one you mean. The food there is very good.'

'You can drive. I'll be responsible for the rest.' He sounded quite buoyant.

The restaurant wasn't busy, so they had no trouble getting a table. They were allotted one near a window overlooking the gardens. The room had a comfortable, elegant atmosphere. The day was bright and full of sunshine. The grounds ran down to the peacefully flowing river. People were out walking with their children and dogs along the bordering trail. There were some chairs and tables out on the terrace, but the tablecloths fluttered in the wind and no one was tempted to sit outside today.

Sharon looked around. 'I like this place. It's never crowded, maybe because it's not directly on a route.'

'I discovered it when I walked along the river path in this direction one day.'

Sharon thought that possibly his weekend dragged. He didn't seem to rush off to a girlfriend, so when he stayed he had to fill in the hours somehow.

Seeing the waiter approaching, Craig told her, 'Whatever you fancy.'

The waiter handed them the menus. They both spent time studying and making their choices. Craig ordered some white wine, and after tasting it, he paused and indicated towards her glass. 'You can afford one glass, even though you're driving. I should have thought of that. We should have gone back for my car.'

She swept his words aside. 'I'm quite satisfied with one glass — or were you hoping to get me drunk?'

He smiled, and his even white teeth flashed momentarily. 'A tempting thought! But heaven forbid!'

He was irresistible: the square chin, the prominent cheekbones, and eyes the colour of slate. He was a very unusual and attractive man. 'So, you've been here before?'

He nodded. 'The food and the service are excellent, and it's very peaceful. That's the biggest drawback in my job — the weekends in a strange place.'

Looking towards the garden, she said, 'Funny, I was just thinking that time must drag for you on occasion.' She couldn't help asking, 'So you don't have a special girlfriend waiting for you to turn up?'

'No, no one special. Not many women put up with just seeing their boyfriends now and then. It's never bothered me much; but until now I've never met anyone who made me want to change my nomadic existence.'

For some silly reason Sharon felt relieved.

He went on, 'Every so often, I've worked seven days a week nonstop.'

'Surely that wasn't necessary?'

'Not necessary; but when everyone disappears on Friday afternoon to their various homes, I'm left adrift till Monday. I can go to pubs, clubs, the theatre or cinema, provided there is one; but if you're on your own it gets tedious. I enjoy reading, but I can't read books twenty-four hours a day either. I plump for long walks or I work nonstop to finish earlier.' The corners of his mouth turned up. 'I'm quite enjoying this particular job. People are very friendly, and the countryside's perfect for long walks. Mildred's cooking is good. Who could ask for more?'

The waiter arrived with Sharon's salad and Craig's soup. Throughout the meal, the conversation flowed and drifted easily. They talked about books and films, about the people in the village, places they'd been, and about hobbies. They shared a love of reading, and Sharon discovered he was particularly interested in history and enjoyed visiting places of historic interest whenever he got the chance.

He asked, 'Do you come from around here?'

With her fork midway, she shook her head. 'I come from Flamborough.'

'Really? My parents took us on a holiday there one summer. My father hoped to get us interested in his hobby of bird-watching, but my brother and I preferred to hike along the cliffs. I remember canoeing around the bay after everyone had made sure I'd be able to cope.' He added, 'We often had a meal in a place called the Rose and Crown. They had large portions and the food was very good. Just what my brother and I needed!'

'The Rose and Crown is still there and still well known for its good food and hospitality. Where do you come from?'

'Enfield. My father is a policeman and my mum works for the local estate agent. When we were small, she worked part-time. These days she works full-time because she says she'd otherwise get bored. She persuaded me to put some of my earnings into my own house, although these days I wonder why.' He ran his hand down his face. 'Admittedly it's now worth twice what I paid for it, but I'm hardly ever at home. My parents keep an eye on it for me. It turned out she gave me good advice, because the collapse of the financial markets meant property was a much better investment than if I'd just stockpiled my money in the bank or invested in stocks and shares. At the moment she's trying to persuade me to buy another flat to rent out.'

Sharon tilted her head to one side and chuckled. 'She sounds very enterprising. I thought you always made up your own mind about taking risks.'

He smiled. 'I do, but she's always handled family finances — something that my father fully approves of — and she gives sensible advice. She made me sceptical about short-term profits. It may be one reason why I ended up doing what I do. I've one married brother. And you?'

'I'm an only child.' Wistfully she added, 'I often wished I had a brother or a sister. I imagine that's much nicer when you're growing up, and all through your life. My father's a teacher and my mum helps out in a local flower shop whenever they're busy.'

They smiled at each other, and Sharon felt very comfortable with him. She could tell he felt relaxed too. Perhaps that was because they were both free from any emotional attachment. They were two people who could spend time together without worrying about the usual kinds of ins and outs, or what the other was thinking all the time. They were both conscious they'd never see each other again once Craig's work was finished. They didn't need to impress each other; they just needed to be and relax.

As the various thoughts whizzed

through her mind, Sharon looked across at him and her heart skipped a beat or two. Apart from his physical attraction, he was also sharp-witted, outgoing and likeable. Normally she had a fondness for men with blond hair and blue eyes, but Craig was an exception. By the time they reached the coffee stage, Sharon admitted without reservation that he was an easy person to be with and like, and they had a lot in common.

Sounding speculative, he surprised her when he asked, 'I was curious about one thing the other evening. Did you go to the Halloween party to improve your standing with people in the factory?'

She shook her head. 'Did it look like that? I hope not. I'm a worker too. I don't want to appear to be a manager who's way above everyone else. I need to keep a certain amount of distance from everyone, and it's up to me who I hire or fire, but I think most people realize I try to be fair. I couldn't do their work and they couldn't do mine.

We're a team. Since I moved to the village, it's quite natural that we meet outside working hours. I think they had problems with that in the beginning, but they've got used to me.'

He nodded. 'You're like the local GP turning up at the pub for a pint. People respect him, but they expect him to realize he'll be treated like everyone else.'

She nodded. 'I don't want people to think I'm Superwoman or special in any way.'

He studied her indulgently. 'I think it's too late for that. A lot of people already do just that, because they know you work hard to keep the factory afloat.'

She coloured and drained her cup. 'That was a delicious meal. Thank you!'

'You're welcome.'

On the way back to the village, Sharon deliberated whether she should invite Craig in for another coffee, but she decided against it. They'd been together for the best part of the day already, and perhaps he wanted to do other things than spend his leisure hours with the manager of the company he was inspecting.

When they drew up outside the pub, he leaned across and unexpectedly kissed her gently on her cheek. Her eyes widened. 'What was that for?'

He grinned. 'Giving me a lift.'

He looked directly into her eyes and she was glad she was sitting. She bit her lip and tried to steady her thoughts. Lost for words, she finally managed, 'Okay. See you tomorrow, then.'

He unfolded himself out of her Mini and nodded before he went towards the pub entrance. Sharon pulled away from the kerb and willed herself not to look back.

7

Arriving early Monday morning, she ran fast-forward on the recorder, but there was nothing suspicious. Sharon didn't like keeping things secret from Gaynor, because they were friends as well as colleagues, but common sense told her she must be impartial. She crossed her fingers and hoped for speedy results.

She spent most of Monday morning bargaining the price for kaolin with a supplier, and felt satisfied with the outcome. After lunch, she heard unusual activity in the outer office and was surprised when she looked up and saw Raymond Keyes talking to Gaynor. Gaynor nodded and pointed towards Sharon's office. He knocked sharply on the door before he came in and gave her a smile. Impeccably dressed in a dark business suit and a pristine white shirt, he held out his hand.

'I had an appointment nearby and decided to call in. After we met at that Halloween party, I thought I should officially call and introduce myself. I'll be pleased to help in any way, at any time. Just get in touch.'

Sharon took his hand briefly. 'Thank you, I will.' At the moment the situation was far too confidential to tell him that someone was stealing and it would affect the annual balance sheet. She must inform the board first, and they had to decide how they wanted to cover the losses — by writing them off as breakages, as manufacturing blunders, or as thefts. Even someone like Raymond Keyes, who was their official accountant and tax adviser, didn't need to be clued up about the present state of affairs yet.

'As I'll be handling your accounts from now on, I'd like to have more insight into the manufacturing process. It'll help me understand better, and perhaps save me asking questions whenever I'm checking.' He looked at his watch. 'It's too late to invite you out to lunch today, but perhaps we can meet another time and talk about the company — where it stands, what it does, and so on?'

Giving him a friendly smile, Sharon replied, 'Yes, by all means. But I don't want to make Sandra jealous.'

'Sandra?' He picked up a pencil and began playing with it. 'Sandra and I are friends. She's fun to be with and very attractive to look at, but no one special. She's a butterfly, flitting from one man to the next. I like her, of course, but I'm just one of many.' He shrugged. 'Suits me! I think she's has her eyes on that chap who's here to analyse company policies.'

Sharon couldn't resist asking, 'And is she making progress?'

He lifted a shoulder. 'Who knows? In my opinion, she's wasting her time. He'll disappear and she'll never see him again. Perhaps she just wants to cut another notch in her stick. What about one day next week for lunch?'

Sharon consulted her desk diary. 'Tuesday or Friday?'

He pulled his phone out of his pocket. 'Tuesday will be perfect. Where would you like to go?'

'The local pub will suit perfectly.'

'Okay, I'll check that they're open and serving lunch.' He extracted a business card and put it on her desk. 'My card, just in case you have to cancel for some reason. I'm generally at main office, but my private details are on it too.'

'Right.' Sharon got up. 'Thank you for calling, and for the invitation, Mr Keyes.'

'Raymond, please!'

She dipped her chin.

'Till Tuesday, Sharon! One o'clock? I'm already looking forward to it.' He turned again at the door to smile at her. When he passed Gaynor, he exchanged a few words with her too.

Something about him bothered Sharon. Although he was friendly and seemingly quite clever, he was too suave, too perfect in his style of dress, and too confident. She also felt there was an air of sexism about him. His comments about Sandra were out of line. A man shouldn't talk his girlfriend down to someone he hardly knew like that.

Her attention was drawn again to her desk diary showing her appointments, reminders, and notes. The coming Friday was circled in red. There was a board meeting. Usually it was fairly informal. She'd have to formulate some relative information and discussion points beforehand, though. She kept the records of what was discussed at the meeting, but didn't note in detail exactly what each member said. Officially Sharon attended because she held ten percent of the shares, and not because she was a manager. Granville held fifty-one percent, and the three other board members shared the remaining ones between them. Slightly disconcerted, she suddenly realized that she hadn't thought about Granville much since they'd parted.

★ ★ ★

When the board members arrived Friday afternoon, they came to Sharon's office. They had nowhere else they could use as a conference room. She cleared her desk, and Gaynor provided coffee and a plate of plain biscuits. Granville came in with the others and sat in her chair, while everyone else grabbed spare chairs. Granville called them to order, greeted everyone in general, and merely looked at Sharon briefly. His expression was withdrawn, his lips parted, his voice curt. He made her feel guilty, even though she had never intended to give him any false hopes. While the others served themselves coffee, he riffled through the notes she had left him on the desk and waited.

He informed the others about the difficulty with supplies of kaolin and that it would decrease profits for a month or two, but that the market was steadying again and their profit margin would increase accordingly. Approval was required to obtain expensive replacement parts for one of the jiggers, and he read a letter from nearby residents about workers blocking the entranceways to their homes with cars.

Walter Johnson shook his head and spluttered, 'Why are people so stupid? It's insolent behaviour, and I don't understand it.'

They agreed to put up a notice on the factory board explaining that there had been official complaints and asking everyone to park in appropriate places, as residents were going to involve the police and the offending cars might be towed away.

Granville passed around a facsimile of a new pattern design that they were initializing in a few weeks' time, and announced that they'd received an order to supply a local restaurant with their own exclusive chinaware. Everyone was satisfied with that news, and then the talk meandered to more general topics that had nothing to do with the company.

Granville wasn't joining in much. His shoulders were hunched. He looked at the papers in front of him and avoided Sharon's glance. It made her feel dreadful. She bit her lip and wished the meeting was over. It did break up several minutes later, and the men began to wander out in ones and twos.

Granville hesitated and held back until they were alone. His blue eyes were questioning and pensive when he turned them to Sharon. 'How are you?'

She swallowed a lump in her throat. 'I'm fine. And you?'

He nodded and studied her face. 'I'm okay. I'm going to London for a while. I may pop over to Paris to see a friend of mine when I'm there.'

'Sounds good. I hope you enjoy yourself.'

He paused for a moment before he said, 'Life goes on, doesn't it?'

She nodded and touched his arm lightly. 'We are still friends, I hope?'

He nodded. 'Of course! I wish we were more than that, but it looks like it's not to be.'

Without waiting any longer, he turned away and caught up with the others. Sharon stared after him. Even if she never met anyone special, she couldn't pretend. A relationship with Granville would have fallen apart in the end because her feelings for him were all wrong.

She rearranged her desk and realized she'd intended to tell Granville about the thefts and how they'd installed a camera, but she'd forgotten all about that when she saw his tense expression. She hoped she wasn't overstepping their legal limits. She'd checked on the internet and found that the use of a hidden surveillance camera for a restricted time was allowed whenever theft was suspected. She made a quick note in her diary to confirm the situation properly with their company lawyer tomorrow, and added a note to inform Granville when he returned.

* * *

Sharon went home on the weekend. She hadn't seen her parents for a while and she enjoyed being spoiled. She went for long quiet walks along the coast. The wind was cold, and the sea was rough with hostile white tops that looked like whipped cream. She returned to the village with bright cheeks and a good appetite.

Driving along the main road late on Sunday afternoon, she saw Craig. He was just about to enter the pub. He looked up as she passed and smiled. She beeped the horn in return.

On Tuesday she arrived punctually for her lunch meeting with Raymond Keyes. He was waiting next to his sports car. She guessed that it was another important factor in his lifestyle.

She got out. 'Nice car. Are you a car fanatic?'

He patted its bonnet and nodded. 'In this day and age, your car is your visiting card. Customers expect you to look the part. And this baby is classy.'

She adjusted her shoulder bag and shrugged. 'It's all a matter of how important it is to you. Men seem to place more importance on what make of car they own than women do. My car gets me from A to B, and as long as it's reliable I couldn't care less if it's candy-pink with blue spots or traditional racing green.'

'A lot of women say that sort of thing, but attitudes are changing. Women are beginning to be pickier.' He reached out and cupped a hand under her elbow. 'Shall we?'

Sharon didn't particularly like the gesture, but she let herself be guided into the pub and into a quiet corner. She hung her jacket on the back of the chair. Mildred was behind the bar and waved to her. There was a pensioner leaning on the bar with his Jack Russell lying at his feet, and two other local men were seated next to the open fire and chatting.

Appearances were clearly very important to Raymond. Today he again looked impeccably turned out, like a mannequin from a window display. 'What can I get you to drink?'

'I'll have a coffee, please.'

'No alcohol?'

She shook her head. 'Not when I'm working.'

'Okay. I'll get myself a lager, and a coffee for you. What would you like to eat? There's chicken and chips, steak and kidney pie, or mango curry.'

'Steak and kidney pie, please.'

He got up again. 'Right, be back in a minute.' He went to the bar to give their order, and Sharon looked around the comfortable room. The horse brasses hanging down the side of the fireplace gleamed in the rays of the sun from the nearby window.

Carrying his lager, Raymond returned. 'Coffee is coming up! And I've ordered our food.'

Sharon leaned back. 'So what would you like to know about the company? You've undoubtedly read last year's balance sheet, so I don't need to explain our financial situation.'

He eyed her and looked a little puzzled. 'No beating about the bush with you, is there?'

'I have to be back at my desk in an hour, so on the assumption that you want to know something about the manufacturing process, this is your chance to ask. I can't tell workers to watch the clock and ignore it myself.'

He took a sip of his drink. 'Tell me about the process of making china, and about marketing and sales.' He eyed her closely, and Sharon felt slightly uncomfortable.

She concentrated on giving him information. 'It would definitely be much easier if you visited and followed the whole process on the spot.'

'Perhaps, but try to explain anyway.'

Sharon kept her explanation simple, but the special jargon associated with

145

the various stages must have gone over his head. He didn't interrupt or ask questions. A short time later, Mildred arrived with their meal and Sharon's coffee. The steak and kidney pie tasted fantastic. Apart from asking if their sales were steady and about any foreign outlets, Raymond remained silent.

When Sharon finished, he said, 'I think I get a fair idea. Tell me about yourself.'

Sharon was startled but too polite to refuse outright. 'What do you want to know? Where I went to university, that sort of thing?'

'No, more personal stuff. What you do in your spare time, what you enjoy doing, where you spend your holidays. I already know that you own Rose Cottage and are renovating it at the moment.'

'Why are you interested?'

'Because you're an attractive woman, and perhaps we'll intensify our friendship one day in the future.' He straightened his tie and waited.

146

She cringed and coloured. 'We have a business relationship, and I hope it remains amiable, but I've no plans for anything else. If I made a play for all the single men connected with my job, I wouldn't have time to do my work.'

'You're going around with Granville Jackson, aren't you? He's part of the company. Perhaps he needs a little competition. It might spur him on.'

Sharon was feeling more uncomfortable by the minute. 'Raymond, it's none of your business. I'm not the type to play off one man against another.'

He grinned and then tried to backpedal. 'No offence intended! I just thought it might be fun for us to go out together sometime — a proper date with candlelight and all the trimmings.'

'I don't think that's a good idea.' She looked at her watch. 'I've got to go. If you need more information, get in touch. You've got the telephone number. Otherwise I presume I'll see you whenever you need to check the accounts.' She got up and grabbed her jacket and her bag before he had much time to react further, stopping briefly to talk to Mildred at the bar. 'The Halloween party was really enjoyable.'

'Glad you liked it.' Mildred eyed Raymond Keyes. 'He's a smooth character, isn't he? I'm surprised to see you with him. He's been in here now and then with Sandra.'

'Oh, it's just a business meeting.'

'That's good. He's not your type at all.'

Sharon asked cheerfully, 'And how would you define my type, Mildred? Any suggestions? Oh, how much was my share of the meal? I don't want Mr Keyes to pay for me.'

Mildred straightened and viewed her carefully. 'You need a gentleman; someone more straightforward. Ten-forty all together, love.'

Sharon handed her the money. 'If you ever think of running a partner service, I might consider being one of your customers.'

Mildred looked more serious when

148

she stated, 'You don't need any help. Men know a good thing when they see it, my dear!'

'Well, I live in hope. Thanks for the meal; it was delicious.'

* * *

Sharon looked at Craig briefly when she passed through the outer office on her return. He was so occupied with his work that he didn't notice her. She hung up her jacket and settled down to her afternoon's work. The meal with Raymond Keyes hadn't encouraged her to want to meet him again, she mused. He had a decidedly pushy attitude and was too interested in her personally. He was also too inquisitive. He was probably the type who thought he was God's gift to women.

Every so often, business associates had tried to date her, but she'd never taken them seriously or wanted to encourage anyone. She was too choosey, too busy settling into her job, and too busy with her cottage renovations to worry about boyfriends and relationships. She'd drifted into her friendship with Granville because he was at hand, and she was glad to share leisure time with someone she liked, but didn't reckon that he'd get serious. Had she been too selfish and a little blind about how he felt? She sighed, pushed her hair off her face, and picked up the phone.

8

Every morning when she arrived, Sharon checked the recording. She had to check it before Gaynor arrived. Gaynor never queried why her boss was suddenly arriving early every day, and assumed it had something to do with her workload.

Sharon waited until Gaynor was out and went to Craig's cubbyhole. He looked up from whatever he was doing and smiled. Her stomach did a somersault. She felt slightly breathless and tried to ignore it.

'Hi there!' he greeted.

'Hi! I just wanted to tell you that I've checked, but there's nothing out of the ordinary so far. I hoped that we'd pin someone down by now.'

He shrugged and his eyes twinkled humorously. 'Be patient! It'd be really unusual to find out who it is so fast. It might take weeks or months.'

With a pleading tone, she uttered, 'Please don't tell me that. I still haven't told Granville what we've done. You haven't mentioned it to him, I presume?'

He shook his head. 'No; it's not my job. You'd better tell him, and also that I helped you to set the camera up. Otherwise he might take offence and say I was interfering in things that had nothing to do with me.'

'I don't think so. Granville is usually very easy-going. Anything that keeps the ball rolling is okay as far as he's concerned. I'll have to tell him soon, though. It's bound to come out eventually, and he and the others might be annoyed if I wait too long.'

Craig shuffled a pile of papers in front of him. 'Yes, I can imagine.'

'Botheration! I still can't quite believe it. You need to be clever to manipulate a system secured by passwords.'

'True, but you'd be surprised at how many people are computer virtuosos these days. Don't give up hope. I expect they thieve according to demand and availability. You need a buyer before it's worth pinching something.'

'I know, but I still find it frustrating. Apart from them messing up the data, they need a key to get into the building, and some kind of transport to get away fast. I can't imagine that they walk out of here on a normal working day with a big box tucked under their arms.'

He shrugged. 'In theory, they could be pinching items now and then, and doing just that. It depends on what they need. Saucers and plates are relatively flat. You could hide those quite easily. You'd need to be more careful when they're bulky items like cups or teapots. I reckon someone clever could pinch a whole coffee set within a week. Naturally, they live in fear of being caught; but you don't check people's bags, do you?'

'No. If we were working with gold, precious stones or the like, I could understand why it might be necessary;

but in a china factory? I think our employees wouldn't like constant inspections, and security checks cost money. People know we have to keep overheads down.'

'Yes; most of the employees I've talked to here are company-orientated and very sensible.'

Sharon knew that he was friendly with Sandra and knew a lot of other local people too by now. She straightened and shrugged. 'I'll just have to wait.'

'I understand why you're worried. You're part-owner, aren't you?'

'Not an important one. I own roughly ten percent of the shares. I'd like more but I'm paying off my mortgage. More share ownership would give me more leverage when making important decisions.'

'This company won't make you a millionaire. I've seen enough of the facts and figures to tell you that already.'

She looked defiant. 'I know that!'

Craig was suitably diverted by her expression. 'I just need to enjoy my work and live comfortably. I'd like to invest in modernizing and new developments, providing we make a steady profit.'

'Which will lead to higher earnings for you personally.'

She countered and smiled. 'Yes, perhaps; but we need to improve this place. Merchandizing, new buildings, better working conditions . . . '

He tilted his head and his eyes sparkled. 'Actually, making money should be your main objective.'

'Do you mean squeezing the last penny out of the firm just to line the pockets of the owner or the shareholders? I know the company has to make a profit — we're not in it for fun — but paying investors a reasonable return and investing for the future should go hand in hand.'

He looked at her tenderly and ran his hands through his hair. 'I like you, Sharon Vaughan. You're unusual.'

She coloured. 'I'd better go make some phone calls. How's your work getting on, by the way? I've never asked.'

'Fine. I've most of the information I need. I expect to be out from under your feet soon.'

'And where will you go then?'

'Not sure. There's a small knitting factory on one of the Scottish isles that looks interesting. I'd quite like to go there. I've never been to Scotland.'

'Can a small knitting factory afford your fees?'

He looked suitably amused again. 'Can a small company like this one afford them?'

Sharon was thinking that the Scottish islands were a long way away, and she'd never see Craig again. She didn't like the idea.

The sound of her telephone interrupted them. She hurried back and settled an enquiry, then looked at her desk diary and thought she ought to phone Granville. He was in all probability back by now.

He sounded quite cheerful. She asked, 'Did you go to Paris as planned? How was it?'

'Yes, and I enjoyed it more than I expected. I met some new people, friends of friends, from the Lake District. They breed horses, so we had a lot of mutual interests. The parents and the two daughters are all enthusiastic riders. I'm going to visit them next week.'

Sharon was glad that he sounded so positive. Perhaps one of the daughters had caught his eye. 'It sounds just up your street.'

'Yes, I think so too. How can I help you?'

'I must inform you about something unusual that's happened at the factory. You'd already left after the last board meeting before I remembered I intended telling you. I don't think it's necessary to inform the others yet, because things are still up in the air; but as you are chairman, I think you should know about it now.'

'Sounds intriguing. What's it about? Fire away.'

Sharon did. She explained how Craig had found the discrepancy during his routine checking and what they'd decided to do. 'He helped me to install a camera, and I'm checking the recording every day to see who's behind it.'

He whistled quietly. 'No one else knows about this?'

'Just me, Craig, and now you.'

'Craig is a decent chap. We can trust him. I imagine in the age of computers that this kind of discrepancy would be easy to spot. Didn't you notice something was amiss?'

She bit her lip. 'I should have, but I didn't compare the production and dispatch figures as often as I should have. I trusted people. I'm sorry, Granville. My fault.'

'Old Haggerty will kick up a fuss when he finds out, but . . . Ah well, I suppose there's no point in crying over spilt milk, is there? Now we need to get to the bottom of this before even more damage is done. I presume we'll have to write off the losses. Do you know roughly how much is involved?'

'I'm only guessing, but I presume it runs into thousands.'

'Wow! We'll keep it between us for now, but we'll have to tell the others at the next meeting. I hope you'll have caught the guilty party by then. These things happen. We'll have to find a way to tighten security though, to make sure that it doesn't happen again in the future.'

'It won't. I'll control the figures more carefully and check that everything balances properly.'

'Okay. Everything *is* okay, apart from the stealing?'

'Yes.'

'Good. Then just keep me informed. I'll be seeing you soon; at the next board meeting at the latest.'

'I'll keep you up to date about the thieving, I promise. Bye, Granville.'

Sharon was beginning to doubt if the

camera helped. Every day she worried about Sam noticing it, and every morning she checked the recorder in vain.

★ ★ ★

Sunday afternoon, after a bout of necessary housework, Sharon decided to go for a walk. She passed the local football pitch, where there was a game in progress between the village team and the neighbouring one. The wind was blustery and cold. She stopped to watch them and pulled her scarf tighter. There were some other onlookers dotted here and there around the pitch, and they were shouting unasked-for advice mixed with scant encouragement. They sounded like they all knew a lot more about the game than the youngsters who were playing.

She jumped when Craig's voice sounded over her shoulder. 'Isn't it too cold for you to be watching that lot?'

She half-turned and declared, 'Anyone

can see they're doing their best. Are you another expert who knows all the answers? Have you actually played football yourself?'

His eyes studied her with a curious intensity. 'I was on the school team.'

'And were you any good?'

Sheepishly honest, he replied, 'No; generally we always got a bashing.'

'And you don't play anymore?'

'Too old, and I'm on the move too much. If I was static long enough, I think I'd enjoy kicking a ball around with a group of oldies.'

Her glance returned to the hectic action on the pitch. 'I must say I admire their guts in this wind. They must be frozen to the marrow. Who's winning?'

Craig thrust his hands deeper into the pockets of his soft overcoat. 'Haven't a clue. I didn't know they were playing today. I just decided to get some fresh air. I've been reading since lunch and thought I needed a break.'

She nodded. 'Like me. I've caught up on my domestic chores for the week, and decided I ought to grab some oxygen before daylight starts to fade.'

'I'll join you, unless you'd rather be on your own. I don't suppose you intend to stand here watching the game, do you?'

Her heart was thumping nineteen to the dozen. 'No, I was thinking of walking down to the river and back.' She glanced one more time at the players and then turned towards the road.

Someone shouted to Craig, and he lifted his hand in acknowledgement before he fell into step.

'You've fitted into village life very fast, haven't you?'

'People are very friendly. The village isn't very big; that's probably why they accept me — they dig for personal information, and that gives them something to pass on to others.'

Sharon glanced across and felt a little breathless as they walked side by side. 'You're right. People are like that around here.' They reached the end of the playing field and she was surprised to see Raymond Keyes getting out of his BMW further down the road. He put his coat on, hurried towards a nearby footpath, and disappeared from sight. She didn't comment, because she wasn't sure whether Craig had noticed him. What brought Keyes to the village on a Sunday afternoon? Sandra?

They walked on with the wind in their faces. After asking her about the camera surveillance, and hearing that nothing had happened, Craig started to tell her about the book he was reading at the moment: a Nordic thriller that sounded quite horrifying. She commented, 'I wonder where authors get their ideas. Perhaps some of them are psychopaths themselves.'

He chuckled. 'I shouldn't think so. I hope not. Information about gruesome murders and the methods they use are in the newspapers every day. Anyone can find detailed medical information on the internet. Human beings are fascinated by horrific situations that no one ever hopes to face in reality.' He tightened his scarf and swept his windblown hair back into place with his fingers.

Sharon had to stop looking at him too often. They reached the old humpback bridge that spanned the river at the end of the village. Modern-day traffic had been diverted to the bypass because the bridge had been built to cater to farmyard vehicles and elegant carriages, not flamboyant cars and trucks. They both came to a halt and watched the water gurgling and gushing over the surface of the rocks and pebbles below.

'I'm already looking forward to some hot chocolate when I get back,' Sharon said. 'It's really cold today, isn't it?'

'Lucky you! I don't think my landlady has hot chocolate.'

She hesitated for a second and then threw caution to the wind. 'Come with me. I've enough for two.'

He studied her and was silent before

he spoke. 'Can't think of anything I'd enjoy more.'

He held out his arm and she tucked hers through the crook of his elbow. They turned back and walked on around the bend. The wind was at their backs now, and Sharon enjoyed feeling almost attached to him.

When they reached her cottage, she disentangled her arm and searched her pocket for her key. He ducked his head as he followed her inside.

'Hang your coat on the hallstand. Go straight ahead to the living room.'

When she joined him, he was studying her multitude of books on the shelves along one wall. She put the tray on a small side table.

He commented, 'You've a nice selection of books.'

'I like trying out new authors. I still haven't got used to e-books; I prefer to hold a real book in my hand. They mount up, though, because I loathe throwing books away. One day I've vowed to sort them out and donate some to a charity shop.'

Craig nodded and took the mug she offered him. She gestured to a comfortable armchair next to the open fireplace, and he sat down. 'I understand why you like real books, but for someone like me, e-books are a blessing. I read a lot, and if I had to carry physical books with me, I'd need another case.' He took a sip and lifted the mug in her direction. 'This is good. Just what I needed.' He looked around. 'I like your cottage. It feels comfortable. You've managed to fill it with the right kind of furniture; small pieces that don't take up too much room.'

'There's still a lot to do. When I moved in, I had the whole plumbing and electrics completely renewed. You can't imagine the mess! It cost a bomb, but I reasoned there was no point in doing bits at a time. I'm now modernizing room by room. The kitchen is finished, as well as the bathroom and the downstairs toilet. This room is almost finished, although

I'm still looking for some rich carpets and some genuine antiques. My bedroom, the former pantry, and the guest rooms upstairs are still all in chaos.'

'You've a pantry? What are you going to do with that?'

'It's too small for most things, but I'm playing with the idea of a shower room. It's next door to the toilet, so the plumbing part of it wouldn't be too difficult. A downstairs shower would be useful because I often come in from the garden with muck up to my elbows. It'd be lovely to pop straight into a shower.'

Craig smiled. 'I can't imagine you with muck up to your elbow. You always look so neat.'

Sharon enjoyed the compliment. 'You can't garden without getting dirty some of the time.'

'Do you like it?'

'Gardening? I didn't like it at all in the beginning. It was a chore, and hard work, because when I moved in the garden was a real wilderness. Since then I've cleaned most of it up, and I learned a little about flowers and plants as I went along. I began to understand that plants died whenever I put them in the wrong place at the wrong time of year. What about you?'

'I've paved the space around my home. I'm never there, so it's the most practical solution. My parents water the tubs of evergreens now and then, and my dad mows the lawn out the back from time to time, so it looks lived-in.'

'It sounds like your house is a waste of your time.'

He shrugged. 'Perhaps it is, but who knows what the future will bring.'

She glanced out of the window. 'I'm going to ask my father to come and help me get rid of that old apple tree trunk at the bottom of the garden. It was already dead when I moved in. I've sawn most of the branches off and got rid of them, but the main trunk is still standing. I'd like to plant a new one in the same spot.'

'That'll be hard work.' He took another sip. 'Don't attempt it on your own. You'll end up in hospital.'

'My dad has some equipment that helps. I don't understand the technicalities, but it involves chains and pulleys and such. Next time they visit, I hope he'll help me get rid of it. I need to decorate one of the guestrooms first, though, so that they have somewhere decent to sleep.'

His eyes twinkled. 'You're a perfectionist, aren't you? I don't suppose your parents mind if they sleep in a half-finished bedroom. They're interested in you and not in your cottage.'

She brushed the hair back off her brow. 'You're right, but a leopard can't change its spots. It just needs a lick of paint, a decent bed, and some decorative touches.'

He met her glance, and Sharon looked down at his long fingers encircling the mug. 'I'd offer to help, but I don't think you'll be doing it next week, will you?'

She listened to his words with a feeling of rising dismay. 'Does that mean you'll be finishing soon?'

'A week or two more and I'll be on my way.'

Her mind didn't want to register the significance of his words. She didn't like the idea that she'd never see him again. It seemed so right that he was part of her world. He was the kind of person who was good to have around. She brushed aside the possibility that he could turn out to be more than that, given more time.

He got up. His looks captured her attention. He was able to stand quite easily, but there wasn't much space between the top of his head and the beams. 'Thanks for the drink.'

Her throat was dry. 'My pleasure. Back to your book again?'

'I expect so. That'll occupy me until the evening meal, and then I'll probably chat with whoever turns up at the pub for a drink until it's time to go to bed.' He turned towards the door and automatically dipped his head a little to pass through smoothly. In the hall, he slipped into his coat and tightened his scarf again.

Sharon could have invited him to share her supper, but she didn't. He might misunderstand. She followed him to the door and held on to the framework with one hand after he'd passed through it. To her surprise, he turned suddenly and drew her form to him. Her body tingled from the contact. His kiss left her wanting more.

'I've wanted to do that for weeks.'

Sharon felt breathless, and barely sensible enough to note that Craig's repeated kiss sent the pit of her stomach into a wild swirl. It was sheer pleasure, and for a few seconds she gave way to its gentle urging and relaxed. When they drew apart, she was totally confused as she looked at him, and coloured faintly like a love-struck teenager. Her legs were decidedly wobbly.

He added, 'Sweet dreams.'

She pulled herself together and answered with a voice full of uncertainty, but which sounded under control. 'If I watch a thriller on TV this evening, I'm more likely to get nightmares.'

He gave a throaty chuckle and his grey eyes sparkled. 'Then don't watch it. Dreams are better than nightmares. See you tomorrow, Sharon.' Without further ado, he lifted his hand above his head and went down the path. Bending to latch the gate, he looked up and gave her another smile before he flicked up the collar on his coat and set off down the road towards the pub.

Sharon stood fixed to the spot. Her fingers wandered across her lips, and she wondered why he'd kissed her. Perhaps it was just a habit. He was continually on the move and met new women constantly. She wasn't the only one who thought he was an attractive man, or who found it difficult to pretend he meant nothing to her. She was just another female among others he met continually.

She was lost in thought for a moment or two, and only resurfaced when goosepimples reminded her she was still standing in the open doorway and Craig was out of sight. About to go inside, a silver BMW speeding past the cottage caught her eye. It looked like Raymond Keyes's car. There was someone else with him, but the car was moving so fast Sharon could barely make out the shadowy figure in the passenger seat.

She busied herself with making something to eat and then switched on the TV, but soon noticed she wasn't the least bit interested in any of the programmes and switched it off again. She tried reading a book, but the silence simply seemed to give her more space to think about Craig, and wonder what he really thought about her and his stay in the village.

9

On Monday morning the office was empty, and as usual the first thing Sharon did was check the recorder. Using the fast-forward button, she was about to delete the whole of the weekend when something caught her eye. She skipped back to the beginning and began to check with care.

On Sunday at ten-thirty, a figure moved across the screen. Even though actually watching someone caught red-handed had been the aim, the sight of them on the premises at a forbidden time flabbergasted her. Deep within, she hadn't wanted to believe any of their employees was capable of stealing. The picture was full of shadows. Whoever it was, they knew their way around the building very well. They didn't bother to switch the light on.

Sharon gazed at the figure as it

approached Sam's desk with a bubble-wrap package in its hand. She guessed from the shape and size that it might be a coffee pot. The shadowy figure shoved it into a bag and turned their attention to the computer on the desk. The figure was hooded, and the angle of the camera didn't show their face. This person was clearly someone who knew what they were doing. After activating Sam's computer, the fingers pounded the keyboard, and seconds later switched it off again. Then they turned away from the camera again.

Sharon knew she was witnessing someone stealing, but was frustrated because she couldn't recognize who it was. The recording was black and white; the surroundings shady. The person was clever enough, or lucky enough, to keep their face hidden. At least they didn't know that a camera was filming them. She leaned back and thought about the next step. She'd wait and talk to Craig about it.

She wrote a note and put it on his

desk, and was just in time. Gaynor came in and started to fuss around with the coffee machine, asking Sharon if she'd enjoyed the weekend. Minutes later Craig arrived. He called his hello in passing and went straight to his desk. Sharon waited for the coffee to brew and then went back to her office with her mug. She looked at him and he gave her a barely perceptible nod.

Later that morning, Gaynor shouted that she was going down to the despatch section to give Sam some orders. She'd barely disappeared when Craig came across. Sharon just mused how familiar his face seemed, and how she'd got used to having him around. With his fingers wound around the edge of the doorframe, he asked, 'What's up? Why do you need to talk to me as soon as Gaynor was out of hearing?'

She explained briefly, and his brows lifted. 'Gaynor will undoubtedly gossip for a while with Sam once she gets there. I thought you'd like to see the film.'

He came in and closed the door. 'Okay, show me what you've got.'

Sharon did. She was intensely aware of Craig's closeness and how he was looking over her shoulder. His looks and the tantalizing freshness of his aftershave captured her imagination and quickened her heartbeat. She was glad that she'd already studied the film, otherwise she might have felt too confused to comment seriously.

He weighed things up in his mind before he stated, 'Pity that the picture isn't clear, but at least you've proof that someone is stealing. They know their way around and where to get what they want. They're also familiar with how to adjust the statistics and cover their tracks. Check, and I bet you'll find Sam's figures were adjusted at exactly the time shown on the video.'

'I haven't done that yet, but I will. You're right — they have it organized down to a T. What should we do next?'

He shrugged. 'I don't recognize who it is either; I couldn't even give an educated guess. It's just someone in a hooded jacket who's taking the maximum precautions not to be recognized. It's almost impossible to see their face, and the bad lighting doesn't help either. It could be a man or a woman. Well, the next step is up to you. Personally I'd keep on filming and hope you'll see more next time.'

'I think it's a woman.' His brows lifted and Sharon rewound the film a little. 'If you look at the hands on the keyboard, they're neat and fairly small.'

He considered the picture. 'You could be right; but some men have artistic fingers, so that's not certain.'

'So we keep on filming?'

He nodded. 'I think it's all you can do at the moment. Maybe we should change the camera's position to get a head-on picture. Let's hope they haven't got all they need yet; then they'll be back for the rest.'

'I still don't understand how they get into the building. They must have a key as well as the computer passwords.'

Craig nodded. 'Looks like it. Why don't you figure out where to position the camera to get a view of their face? I'll move it for you after everyone's left this evening.'

Her thoughts circled around Craig, how he kissed her last Sunday, and how helpful he was. 'Yes, thanks; I will. I've lived in dread that Sam would spot the camera ever since we put it there, but it seems we're not finished yet. Oh, I'd better phone Granville and put him in the picture.'

There was silence and then he sounded very detached. 'Granville? Oh, yes, by all means. I'd better get back to my desk before Gaynor returns and wonders what we're chatting about.' He walked towards the door. 'Let me know about moving the camera and the best time to do it. I can always come back later to fix it if you like.' With his hand on the door handle, he added. 'Regards to Granville.'

Sharon watched him walking briskly

back to his cubbyhole and she wondered whether she'd done something to bother him. He wasn't a moody person, but his expression hadn't been encouraging. He looked distracted. Perhaps he was fed up with being involved. She hoped she wasn't annoying him.

Sharon picked up the phone and tried to contact Granville, but he wasn't at home. The housekeeper told her he was visiting people in the Lake District and wouldn't be back until Thursday. Sharon remembered he was visiting the family he'd met in Paris. She had his mobile number, but wouldn't bother him with business. This wasn't an emergency, and perhaps she'd be able to give him more information next time they spoke. She might even be able to tell him they'd caught someone red-handed.

During the course of the day, she thought about where to put the camera. Craig phoned her just before he left that afternoon. 'And?' he said.

'We'll reposition it.'

'Okay. What time do you want me to come back?'

'Is six all right with you?'

'Fine. I'm in the darts team tonight. That starts at roughly seven-thirty, but they won't miss me if I'm not there dead on time.'

'If we meet at six, you'll be back on time. It didn't take you long to position the camera last time.'

'Right. See you outside at roughly six then?'

'Yes.' She paused. 'And thanks, Craig. I don't know how I'd manage without you.'

'You would, I'm sure.'

When she finished for the day, she checked the area near Sam's desk. The factory was closed for the day and most people had left, although the ovens were firing overnight. If anyone asked what she was doing, she'd make an excuse and move on again.

She noticed there was a shelf above Sam's desk full of thick files. Some were standing, while others were lying flat on

181

top of each other. She craned her neck to see what was on their labels and found they were copies of records of company sales from the pottery's first year. She reckoned that no one was likely to need them anymore as everything was stored on their computer system. Provided Craig could place the camera between the files and aim it towards the computer — they'd get a first rate close-up.

She stuffed an empty sheet of paper from a nearby pile into her shoulder bag, in case someone was watching, and left. The building was almost empty, and Billy, the caretaker, would soon be switching off lights and checking the doors were locked before he left.

Sharon went home and made herself a quick meal. She drove back in the direction of the factory just after six and parked in a street near the playing field. Remaining alert in case she met someone, she strolled into the yard and unlocked the entrance door, leaving it slightly ajar. Craig arrived minutes later. He was wearing jeans and a dark blue checked shirt under his anorak. Sharon wished she wasn't so vulnerable to his attractions.

She suddenly realized she was falling in love with him. He was someone she hadn't even known a few weeks ago, and he would disappear out of her life as quickly as he'd come, but that didn't prevent her from loving him. She cleared the lump in her throat and gave him a forced smile. 'Punctual as usual.'

He stuck his hands into the pockets of his jacket. 'Have you thought about where to put the camera?'

Sharon re-locked the door and set off immediately for the despatch section. Over her shoulder she said, 'Yes; I checked earlier. I think we could place it between some obsolete files. Come and take a look.'

He followed her and their footsteps echoed through the empty rooms. When they reached Sam's desk, he agreed with her choice. 'I'll get a stepladder and the camera. I'll conceal it as carefully as I can. Go upstairs. When I've moved the camera, you should be able to see the result.'

Upstairs in her office, Sharon loaded the recorder with an empty tape and kept the old one with the indistinct pictures of the unknown thief, in case they never got anything better. She waited, and after a while the picture wobbled and showed various things like the shelving and the floor as Craig placed the camera in a new position on the shelf. His face was close up, and Sharon felt a flutter in her abdomen as she studied his features.

Finally he climbed down, and she could tell he'd chosen a good position. A minute or two later he came into her office and looked over her shoulder. Her heart hammered wildly. She hoped he wouldn't notice.

He nodded. 'That looks good. Or do you want me to adjust it again?'

She shook her head. 'It's perfect.'

'Start the recording and come to check how it looks from Sam's chair. If it's okay, we can both go home.' He gave her a smile that sent her pulse winging.

Sharon followed him downstairs and saw that the camera was cleverly hidden. Sam would never notice it. How often did he or anyone else glance up there? They put the lights out and went outdoors. Daylight was fading fast.

'Would you like a lift back to the pub?' Sharon offered.

Craig laughed. 'I can already imagine the questions that'll be fired at me in the pub as soon as someone sees me in their boss's car at this time of day. They're always looking for something new to gossip about.'

She chuckled. 'It's not midnight! You could have been working late, and I had to go back for something I forgot. You have to use your imagination and keep them guessing. I can drop you off nearby if you like.'

'I'd have to squeeze myself into your sardine tin and prise myself out again.

It's quicker for me to walk.'

She sniffed. 'Stop insulting my car. I love it. It's not my fault that you're the wrong size and shape.'

He considered her for a moment, his face was pensive. 'See you tomorrow?'

'Yes. Is the darts team playing against each other, or is it an inter-village thing?'

The wind played with his hair. 'I don't really know. Bert coerced me onto the team along with some locals, including some men from the pottery. I'm not a darts enthusiast, but it passes the time. Pity — you don't play darts, do you?'

She shook her head. 'I am life-threatening to anyone within a radius of a mile. Enjoy yourself!'

'I'll try.' He eyed her for a moment and pushed his windswept hair to the side. 'What are you planning this evening?'

'Nothing much. I think I'll call on Bob Wilson on the way home. After that, there's the mind-numbing prospect of ironing, television or reading.

Actually there's a historical serial on this evening about the House of Lancaster I'd like to see.'

'Who's Bob Wilson?'

'One of our kiln workers. He's been ill for several weeks with chest trouble, and he's bored to tears. He needs to be one hundred percent fit to do his job.'

'And it's your duty to visit him?'

'I don't have to, but I like doing that kind of thing. Bob and his wife live close by and they have no children. Other people in the village keep an eye on them too. They're lovely people. Bob is due for retirement next year.'

He tilted his head to the side. 'This really is an unusual company. I thought visiting sick employees went out with the dodo.'

'I don't visit everyone — only the ones I particularly like, and when they're sick for a long time.'

His eyes twinkled. 'Probably that means ninety-nine percent of them.'

She tossed her head. 'I admit that I like most of the people who work for us. Anyway, Bob's wife makes delicious cake, and she usually gives me a piece with a cup of tea.'

Craig was silent for a moment, and then he declared, 'I thought you were unusual from day one. You're quite unique.'

Sharon was glad that the nearest lamp-post was further down the street, and the light was sparse where they faced each other. He couldn't detect how she coloured or how much his words warmed her heart.

'Bye then!' he said.

She nodded. 'Thanks again, Craig.' They parted and went in opposite directions.

A few moments later, Sharon passed him in her car. She beeped the horn, and he lifted his hand in reply.

* * *

The next morning, she immediately checked the recording. There wasn't anything unusual. The first scenes showed her with Craig adjusting the camera above Sam's desk. She was tempted not to erase that; she'd love to have some pictures of Craig. But when she studied the scene again, she erased it all with a heavy heart. Leaning back into her chair, she already felt a sense of loss, and her heart ached. They'd never even kissed passionately in the way she dreamed about, but she knew that she loved him.

Too many people these days seemed to base their relationship on erotic, physical attraction, and that was why they habitually floundered and failed. They married in haste and regretted at leisure. When she imagined what being in love with someone was like, she thought it should be a feeling of finding a soulmate as well as someone she felt was alluring. Love based on respect and real friendship was more likely to survive these days than spontaneous attraction. She'd read somewhere that the essence of marriage shouldn't be sex, or money or even children: it should be commitment.

She'd never met anyone before who came close — until Craig. He was fun to be with, and intelligent, but she also had a feeling he could be unrelenting and determined whenever he thought it necessary. She automatically felt more alive and vibrant whenever he was close. She wanted him, even though she knew he was leaving soon and she'd never have the chance to get to know him better. She would carry on with her life without him; but if she had a fairy to grant a wish, she'd ask her to make him fall in love with her. He made friends easily, even though his job meant he often began facing hostilities. He had the knack of being likeable and pleasant with the very people he was analysing for his final reports. He was quite special. She sighed as her thoughts continued to centre on him until she reached Bob Wilson's cottage.

★ ★ ★

On Thursday, Gaynor and Craig arrived together. When Sharon went to get her first cup of coffee, he was stuffing papers in his briefcase. He joined them briefly at the coffee machine and gave her a questioning look, and Sharon understood he was curious about the camera's recording. Sharon shook her head.

'I'm going to headquarters for a day or two to discuss my report,' Craig announced.

Sharon listened and her heart sank. She gripped her mug more tightly and told herself it was good training for the time he'd permanently disappear from their lives.

Gaynor asked him, 'Will you be back next Sunday? Ken and I were thinking of going to the Whinlatter Forest Centre. There's a restaurant where we could have a coffee break and there are good walking tracks. There are also some spectacular views across the fells and forests of the northern lakeland. We went there two or three years ago and enjoyed it so much that we were determined to go back one day. We were thinking of next Sunday. The weather forecast is good, and there won't be so many other visitors at this time of year. Are you doing anything, Sharon?'

'Next Sunday? No, I'd like to come. My alternative is clearing the garden for the winter.' She smiled. 'Your suggestion is a lot nicer.' Sharon was glad she could accept before Craig had time to reply. She didn't want anyone to think he had influenced her decision. Secretly she thought another outing with Craig would be a great memory to store away for the future when he was no longer around.

'What about you, Craig?' Gaynor said.

He shrugged. 'If talks drag on, I may not be able to get away.'

'Well, it's an open invitation. Let us know. Whinlatter is worth a visit.'

He smiled. 'Will do!' He grabbed his briefcase and left.

Half-listening to Gaynor's chatter, and sipping her coffee, Sharon was hoping he'd make it in time. She shook her thoughts and realized she wasn't concentrating on work properly these days. She slept uneasily, and thought too much about Craig and how he'd changed things ever since he'd arrived.

★　★　★

On the following Monday morning, she checked the video film and was shocked. This time the thief was directly facing the hidden camera. It was Sandra! Sharon stared at the screen for a moment before she collected her thoughts, and wondered what came next. How would Craig feel when he discovered Sandra was the thief? Did he like her enough to interfere and try to block any further action? There was no doubt who it was — one of their own painters. How had she got in, how did she know the passwords, and where was she trading the goods?

There was no point in confronting her yet, Sharon decided. Direct accusations were pointless. She had a video of Sandra in the factory, but was that enough? She was an employee and could lie about why she was there. Sharon stopped the recording and leaned back in her chair. Gaynor breezed into the office with her usual good humour and started her usual routine of making coffee. Sharon joined her. She needed time to think about her next step. She was still flummoxed, but if Gaynor noticed anything unusual in her manner, she didn't say so.

Gaynor said, 'Craig phoned last night. He thinks he'll be back in time to come with us on Sunday.'

Sharon's heart lightened. 'Will he? That's good.'

'Yes, I think so too. He's a nice chap, even though his job is investigation.'

'I don't think he'd like being called an investigator. That would put him in the same category as Sherlock Holmes, and he told me he thought the recent

194

TV series was not up his street!'

Back in her office, Sharon presumed Craig would be shocked to find the culprit was Sandra, but she knew enough about him already to guess that even if he were having an affair with her, it wouldn't stop him blaming or accusing her. Perhaps she should inform Granville? But he'd call the police instantly, and then Sandra would close up like a clam and they'd never find out how she'd got the passwords or the key. They could change every password in the company; but with a possible rogue element in the firm, the same thing could happen again in the future.

Craig understood the ins and outs of the business world and the present situation. He was sensible and calm. Sharon was sure he'd rally round and help her. She couldn't help the fact that he might be disillusioned by Sandra's behaviour. She'd wait and talk to him when she could, Sharon decided.

★ ★ ★

Gaynor phoned on Sunday morning to tell her Craig would be driving, and they'd be coming to pick her up just after lunch. She waited expectantly, glancing nervously out of the living room window. She told herself it was just another trip like any other, but she knew she was kidding herself. Craig was with them, and that made it special. She even pushed her camera into her bag. It might be the last innocent possibility to take a couple of photos of him.

When he arrived, Sharon grabbed her things and hurried out. Ken was sitting in the front, and she got into the back with Gaynor. She felt a warm glow flow through her as Craig turned around to smile and say hello. It was barely a couple of days since she'd last seen him, but it seemed like an eternity. She felt blissful and fully alive again, astonished at the sense of fulfilment she felt from just being with him. What had become of the sensible, level-headed woman who planned in advance and considered every move she made? If she knew Craig wanted her, she'd throw caution to the wind and go with him without thinking twice.

She tried concentrating on Gaynor's news about Saturday's shopping trip and about the boys' latest test results. Ken gave Craig directions, and Sharon heard with half an ear as the two men also chatted about the football results. She had to drag her attention back to Gaynor and murmur suitable replies.

As Gaynor had foretold, there were hardly any walkers or mountain bikers, and the ones they did see soon went off in other directions. The signposted walks began and ended near the visitor centre. They set out and found the paths were marked with numbered posts at any intervening junctions, so they could enjoy their surroundings and amble along the right route. Most of the time everyone was silent.

A short time later, they reached a

spectacular view across the fells and the forest. Gaynor had a flask of coffee in her backpack, and they made themselves comfortable on some convenient rocks to enjoy it and chat about the district. Ken and Gaynor set off again before Craig and Sharon were quite finished. The well-marked route would lead them back to the centre, so there was no risk of anyone getting lost.

Because they were alone, Sharon felt like a giddy teenager. 'How did your visit down south go?' Craig was close; so close that it almost took her breath away when she looked into his grey eyes. They twinkled, and his expression was humorous. Breezes were blowing his hair haywire, and Sharon had an urge to kiss him.

'Good! It took less time than I expected. My boss checked things and approved.'

'So that means you're almost finished here?'

'Yes. I've got to knock the text into shape, but it's finished, and I can think about my next task somewhere else.' He watched her carefully for a moment before his glance returned to the surrounding scenery. 'Quite impressive here, isn't it?'

She nodded without replying. The fact of his imminent departure twisted and turned inside her like a knife. She needed to think of other things, and decided that she would tell him about the video recording. 'I'm glad to get you on your own for a few minutes.'

'Are you?' He tilted his head to one side and grinned. 'For improper reasons?'

'Don't be silly. This is serious.'

He straightened and took another sip of coffee. 'Fire away! What's bothering you?'

She told him, and he whistled. She added, 'I'm sorry that it's Sandra. I know you and she are friends. It's not a nice situation for you.'

'Do you think Sandra is special to me in some way? She isn't.' He shrugged dismissively. 'Looks are often deceptive.

Sandra thinks she can use hers to get whatever she's after.'

Sharon swallowed. 'Then I'm glad, because it'll make it easier for us to decide what we have to do.'

'We? It's your task, not mine.'

She shoved her hair off her forehead with one hand. 'I know, but you found the discrepancy in the first place. You helped me with the camera; and I do value your opinion. Granville would just dial nine-nine-nine. I need to find out about how she knew the passwords before I involve the police. I'm not sure if our recording could be used in court. I was thinking she could easily lie and say she was in the factory for some other reason.'

Craig threw the dregs of his coffee into the nearby greenery. 'I see what you mean. Yes, it's undoubtedly better to catch her red-handed with a witness. For what it's worth, I suggest you keep an eye on her for a day or two and make discreet enquiries about her friends. I don't think she can pull it off on her own. She must have a helper and a buyer. The china is expensive, so it's destined for an upper-class wholesaler or retailer. Sandra works five days a week, and she seems to spend most of her weekends locally. I don't think she owns a car, either.'

Sharon bit her lip. 'Yes, I see what you mean. I don't know who she goes around with, and I can hardly start asking personal questions. People will wonder why.'

'You'd be surprised how much people reveal when you drop names casually at the right moment. I'll ask around if you like. People in the pub are often prepared to gossip without noticing what they're doing. In the meantime, keep using the camera. Have you figured out what she's pinching at present? She might need to try again soon.'

'I checked stocks and compared them to what's been sold in the last two weeks. I think she's collecting a coffee service, the one with the gold rim.' She paused. 'Why is she doing it? Her wage is above average. Why put your job in danger by stealing from your employer?'

'Well, whatever the reason, I bet she's not collecting stuff for her bottom drawer. She's tempted, and she's prepared to take the risk for money on the side or some other reason we don't understand.'

'It's still hard to believe. All the workers get reduced prices when they want to buy something. We limit the amount they can buy, but she could buy and resell at a profit.'

'Well that's not enough, by the look of things. Just watch her and wait for the next development.'

'I'll need definite proof before I involve the police.' Sharon paused and continued, 'I might even spend the night in the office at the weekend. Perhaps I'll catch her at it red-handed.'

'You've no guarantee she's alone in the building. Things could get nasty. If you intend to stay in the office overnight, tell me and I'll come too. I'm sure there must be someone else involved. Sandra is most likely the dupe. She does the stealing, and someone else pockets most of the money.'

Sharon bit her lip and nodded. 'Yes, that's quite likely.'

He paused. 'What about Granville?'

'I'd like to have more definite evidence before I tell him. Thanks, Craig — I had a feeling you'd help me find the right way to go about this.'

He made a sweeping gesture with his hand. 'My pleasure. It's nice to know you trust me so much.' He took a visiting card out of his pocket and handed it to her. 'Do you have my private number? Remember, don't try staying overnight in the office on your own. That's not a good idea.'

She stuffed the card in her pocket and tried to turn the conversation in a new direction. 'How was your trip home, otherwise — apart from business?'

'Okay. I called to see my parents,

checked the house, and even had time to visit my brother. It also gave my mother the chance to ask about girlfriends and when I intend to settle down, but I'm used to that by now.'

Sharon chuckled and her eyes twinkled. 'My mother is the same. She's been asking me about my 'knight in shining armour' since I was about fifteen.'

Their glance locked, and there was a moment of silence before he leaned towards her and kissed her gently on her lips. Her expression was startled as he straightened and commented, 'Too much of a temptation. Shall we go?' He reached out and he pulled her up. Reluctantly, she freed herself and hid her confusion. He stared at her and shoved his hands deeper into the pockets of his anorak.

Sharon was still breathless, but she straightened and gave him a shaky smile before finally turning away and heading towards the path. She tried to concentrate on merely enjoying the rest of the day. They had to walk in single file most of the way back. Craig and Sharon were silent, each of them busy with their own thoughts. By the time they caught up with Ken and Gaynor, Sharon had recovered and could pretend normality again. They stopped briefly for coffee and sandwiches at the visitor centre.

There weren't many other visitors, and when they set off home daylight was fading. Ken and Gaynor didn't notice that the other two were quiet. Craig drove into the village and halted at Sharon's cottage. She invited them all in, but Gaynor and Ken wanted to get home, and Craig remained silent. After her goodbyes, and with her key in the lock, she listened to the sound of his car fading into the distance.

10

Sharon decided to keep Granville up to date and hoped that he wouldn't interfere. He was entitled to know. She rang him.

'Sharon! How are you?'

'I'm fine thanks. And you?'

'Great! Great!' There was a bounce to his voice. He sounded like the old Granville. 'What can I do for you?'

Sharon explained that Sandra was the thief and that they now intended to catch her red-handed before they took any further steps.

He breathed out loudly. 'I can't say that the name means anything to me, but I expect if I saw her I'd recognize her. Why do people do these things?'

'That's what I've asked myself too.'

'I gather you don't want to go to the police yet?'

'We may have to eventually, but it'd

be sensible to try and discover who her partners in crime are first. Craig said he'd help me.'

'Craig? Oh, yes — he's helped from the beginning, hasn't he? Jolly good of him.'

'Yes, he's been very supportive.

There was a short pause. 'What are you planning?'

'Spending the weekend in the office and catching her in the act. That way we may be able to frighten her into telling us where she got the keys and the passwords.'

'Oh, yes. I hadn't considered that aspect . . . I see what you mean. If we don't know how she's getting in, we'll have to change all the locks. Surely it's quite simple to change the passwords.'

'But if she has a partner in the company and we throw her out, they could find out the new passwords and use them in some way, like selling sensitive information to our rivals. We need to sort this out and close the security gap.'

'Hmm, I see! Well, don't wait too long before involving the police, and don't do anything silly. What about filming employees without their knowledge? Is that okay?'

'I've checked that, and our legal firm thinks that under the circumstances we're safe.'

'If she doesn't turn up, I suggest you confront her with the recordings you have and threaten her with the police.' Sharon heard him rustle some papers. 'She'll possibly get off on probation, but we must dismiss her no matter what happens.' He cleared his throat. 'I intended to phone you, as a matter of fact. I wanted to give you prior warning that I'm selling my company shares.'

The breath caught in Sharon's throat. 'What? All of them?'

'Yes. I know it's a bolt out of the blue, but I've decided to invest money in breeding horses, and most of my other assets are fixed. I can't liquidate anything else without creating complications. Previous generations have tied up our money in land and things like long-term bonds or government stocks.'

'But . . . assuming you pull out, the company will go downhill overnight. As soon as people notice you're selling, they'll think there's something wrong.'

'Sharon, don't panic! It won't happen overnight, and no one else knows what I intend to do yet. I'll offer them to the other board members first. You can even buy them yourself if you like!'

Sharon considered her present financial position. She couldn't afford to buy more than another ten percent. 'I won't pretend I'm not shocked. I never reckoned with something like this. The company's doing well.'

'I know that. In fact, Craig's preliminary report is positive, and I'm sure once it's made public it'll allay anyone's doubts. I don't like doing it, Sharon.'

'Has this anything to do with us and our friendship?'

'No, of course not. I'm not petty-minded. You were right; a close long-term relationship wouldn't have worked. Our interests would clash. I was depressed for a while until I met Vanessa.'

'Vanessa?'

'Remember how I told you I was going to Paris and how I met a family there? They breed hunters in a big way. Vanessa is their daughter, and I fell for her hook line and sinker. Amazingly, she feels the same way about me. I decided it'd be a great idea to start an additional breeding stable at my place. I've got the staff and the space. It means rebuilding parts of the stables and investing in breeding stock. That's an expensive undertaking, and that's why I need the extra money.'

Sharon pushed the hair off her forehead. 'I'm glad that you've found someone you like so much, but are you sure you're doing the right thing? I know nothing about horses, but it sounds like a risky undertaking to me.'

His voice was still bouncy. 'I already know a lot about horses, Sharon, and

I'm willing to take the chance. Vanessa and her parents will help and advise. I'd like to do it.'

She tried to feel happy for him. 'Then I wish you luck. I'm really glad for you about Vanessa and hope that we'll stay friends.'

'We will, I'm sure. You must come to dinner one evening and meet her. I think you'll like her. She's quite wonderful.'

Sharon wasn't so sure. She wasn't on the same wavelength as most of Granville's friends. Nearly all of them came from equestrian circles or were landed gentry. 'You'll let me know when you intend to sell?'

'Yes, of course. Everything is still at the planning stage at the moment.' He paused. 'Try to sort out this thieving business so that it doesn't cast an additional shadow on things when I put up the shares. I'll reassure the other board members and tell them to hang on to their shares, or even buy mine if they have any spare cash, because with you at the helm the company does have a rosy future.'

A few minutes later, Sharon still felt slightly shocked when she considered Granville's news. When new shareholders took over, it might mean a continuous wrangle with people who knew nothing about production methods or anything else to do with the firm. She straightened her shoulders. She'd contact her bank manager tomorrow and find out whether he was willing to stretch her credit.

She didn't sleep well that night. The knowledge that Craig was thinking of immediate departure, and today's news that Granville was selling his shares, made sleep simply impossible.

* * *

The next day, Craig was busy elsewhere and Sharon didn't see him before she left for a hastily arranged appointment with her bank manager. As she expected, he wasn't prepared to extend

212

her credit beyond a reasonable level.

'You already have a mortgage on your cottage, and you chose a shorter repayment method. There's no way for you to adjust that within the first ten years. I'm prepared, of course, to endorse some additional credit, but I can't agree to an excessive figure. You seem to need an amount far beyond what I can allow.'

Sharon nodded. 'I thought so. You know that I own ten percent of company shares. I want to buy some more.'

His forehead wrinkled and he looked at her speculatively. 'I take it you know that more are coming onto the market in the near future?'

'Yes. I hope you'll treat that knowledge with absolute secrecy. I just wanted to find out how many I can afford to buy.'

He nodded. 'Of course; that goes without saying. Our customers must be able to trust us implicitly. Whatever you tell me remains within these four walls.

In six or seven years' time, your financial situation will be quite different. I'm afraid my superiors will fall on me like a ton of bricks if I endorsed a large credit margin for you at present.'

Sharon stood up and extended her hand. 'I understand. I didn't really expect any other answer. Thank you anyway.'

On the way back to the office, her thoughts circled around the future. She considered, and then rejected, appealing to her parents for a loan. She hoped for her own sake, and for all the employees', that whoever bought the shares would be sensible and sympathetic.

Craig was in his office, and she managed a wave and a smile. He lifted his hand. She grabbed a mug of coffee on the way and concentrated on bargaining with one of their suppliers.

Craig stuck his head round the doorway when Gaynor was out. Sharon looked up. 'Everything okay?' he asked. 'You look very pale this morning.'

214

She gave him a hesitant smile. 'Do I? I didn't sleep very well. I've decided I'll come in on the weekend and try to catch Sandra red-handed. I've told Granville. He doesn't want to wait much longer before we involve the police, so it's this weekend or nothing.'

He nodded and ran his long fingers through his dark hair. 'Okay. Just tell me when you intend to come and I'll join you.'

She lifted her hand in a weak protest. 'You don't have to, Craig. This is my problem, not yours.'

'As I mentioned the other day, it's too risky for you to be on your own.'

She smiled jovially. 'And how will you explain your absence to Mildred at the pub?'

He gave her a lopsided grin. 'She's used to me coming and going. Luckily, I access my room via the outer staircase. They never know whether I'm there or not. Once I've had my meal, I often disappear for the rest of the evening.'

She studied his features, which seemed so familiar and dear, and nodded. 'Okay, if you insist. I intend to start watching on Friday evening. I'll go home as usual and bring some sandwiches back with me. Unfortunately, there's just one hard bench-like fixture in our first-aid room downstairs. We only have chairs up here.'

'We'll manage. I'll join you after my meal. We can take it in turns to go home and freshen up. If Sandra hasn't turned up by teatime Sunday, we'll call it a day.'

She exclaimed, 'This is a bit like James Bond and MI5, isn't it? Spying and trying not to be caught in the process.'

'Not quite as exciting though. They chase spies and terrorists. We're after a china thief.'

Gaynor's steps sounded on the metal stairs and he turned back to his office without another word. That was something else that bothered Sharon a lot. She wanted to tell Gaynor what was going on. She would, first thing on Monday, no matter what happened.

* * *

Sharon was away from the office for the two following days in Manchester, negotiating with a catering firm for a contract. After a lot of persuasion, haggling and bargaining, she was successful and they signed. She returned to the factory pleased with the result. Their designer had come up trumps, and Sharon knew that sometimes one contract led to another. Driving back, she decided to contact shipping companies, hotels and the like. Sometimes smaller companies like theirs were more successful than famous ones because they were more flexible and eager to please.

She heard that Craig had been in and out of the office all week. He'd told Gaynor he was busy confirming and formulating his final report. He'd been to visit Granville one day, and had left the next morning to talk to his own bosses again. Sharon wondered if he'd be back in time to help her keep watch.

He phoned her on Thursday and said he'd be back Friday afternoon and would meet her after office hours at the company. The mere sound of his voice produced butterflies in her chest. Although the reason for meeting was serious, she looked forward enormously to spending time with him again. Perhaps this was the last chance for her to be on her own with him.

She often wished she had an airy office with lots of windows, but her present room merely had a single small window that overlooked a narrow alleyway at the back of the building. She'd never seen anyone in the passageway, and the window was almost invisible from below and from the road, so they'd be able to use the desk light.

She went home as usual on Friday afternoon. Making sandwiches, grabbing a torch, and gathering some magazines and a book she was reading, she shoved it all into her briefcase. She waited an hour before she took a roundabout route back to the firm, and checked no one was in sight before she slipped inside.

She had barely made herself comfortable when she heard muffled knocking downstairs. It could only be Craig. Sandra had a quieter method of getting in. Sharon hurried to let him in. They grinned at each other and after she'd relocked the door.

He took off his coat and pronounced, 'I've just had chicken pie. I told Mildred I was tired and having an early night.'

'Good. I've brought some sandwiches. We'll almost certainly get very bored. I hope it's worth the effort.'

He shrugged. 'Let's hope for the best.' He studied her for a moment. 'You look better today.'

Flustered that he took any notice of how she looked, she answered, 'You mean the day when I told you I hadn't slept well?'

There was a moment of silence. 'Granville told me that he was selling his company shares.'

'Did he?' She sat down. 'Yes, it gave me a bit of a shock. I just hope whoever buys the controlling shares will let me go on running things.'

'Would you mind much if someone wanted to interfere with your management?' He paused. 'That's a stupid question. Of course you would.'

She gestured to another chair. 'I could even lose my job; but if the pottery goes downhill, it'll be much harder for the workers. They have families to support. Granville is entitled to do what he likes, of course. He's decided to invest in something quite different.'

Craig nodded. 'I thought you had more influence over him. His investment in the factory gives him a steady income. Breeding horses is a risky long-term investment.'

'I've no idea what breeding horses entails, but I presume he's thought things through. He doesn't generally take chances; and if things did go wrong with this horse-breeding scheme, he has plenty of other sources of income. He mentioned you've given us a positive ruling in your preliminary report?'

'Yes. I've stated that the company has prospects. There are a few weak points in the general set-up, but on the whole you're doing well. I've made some suggestions about future developments, and about small changes that might be beneficial.'

'Can I see it?'

He shook his head. 'Sorry, but I have to let Granville have the final report before anyone else — company rules — but you'll be next in line. I always try to keep my word.'

She nodded. 'I understand. I'll look forward to reading it.' She opened the drawer and switched the recorder on. 'I still believe I know what's good for the company better than anyone else.'

He looked at her for a moment and

said, 'You'll fight for the company and the employees to your last breath, even when things seem hopeless, won't you?'

She met his glance and smiled. 'Of course. I just hope I don't make too many mistakes.'

'You're getting the best possible results. You're doing fine.'

She coloured and fidgeted with an arm of the chair. 'I'm going to make some coffee. Want some?'

He nodded. 'We may as well make ourselves comfortable.' He reached forward for her newspaper. 'I hope you've got card games on your computer? It's going to be a long night.'

'Officially, no I don't. Unofficially, yes I do. Some card games and mahjongg! I'll get the coffee.'

They chatted quietly about all kinds of things. They thought on similar lines and differed seldom, apart from how to handle some recent chaotic politics. Time passed faster than Sharon expected because they were both busy chatting and listening to each other. Nothing unusual happened. Sharon kept stretching her back, and eventually Craig said, 'Why don't you go to sleep? I'm okay. I'll keep my eye on the recording for a while.'

She laid her head on the desk and tried to sleep but it didn't work, even with her jacket folded into a pillow. She must have dozed off eventually, though, because she opened her eyes when Craig shook her gently.

'I've been down to the first-aid room and pinched the mattress,' he said. 'It's on the floor over there. I found a blanket too.'

She glanced across at the mattress. 'It's tempting, but it's not fair on you.'

'I'm fine. I'll play cards until I drop off. I don't think someone will try something in the middle of the night. Nothing unusual has happened so far.'

She gave in. Even the hard surface felt heavenly because she could stretch out. She pulled the blanket up to her chin and was asleep in minutes. Craig looked at her and grinned. He spread his coat on top of the blanket for extra warmth.

11

The first weak signs of daylight were struggling through the undersized window when Sharon woke. She checked her watch and looked at Craig. He was hunched over her desk with his head on his folded arms. She felt guilty. She got up and he heard her. He stretched, swivelled around and rubbed the back of his neck.

'Craig! You should have woken me hours ago.'

'What for? I'm almost certain nothing happened, but you can check the video just in case.' He yawned and ran a hand over his face. 'I'm going back to the pub. I'll have a wash and a shave and eat breakfast, then tell Mildred I'm going out on a trek. She'll make me some sandwiches, and I'll come back. Then it's your turn to go for a while. As long as one of us watches, it'll be fine. Are you hungry?

If you are, you can go first.'

She shook her head. 'No, I'm fine. I can't pretend that I've had the best night's sleep ever, but it was better than yours. Off you go!'

He rubbed his shadowed chin, made coffee, and handed her a mug. 'You've got my number. Ring as soon as anything unusual happens. Promise?'

She laughed softly. 'Yes, promise! I'll let you out and give you the key. Take your time. Take a nap! I'll be fine.'

Their eyes met and his expression was wistful. 'Okay. And don't try anything hare-brained.' He shook his coat and put it on before he followed her downstairs. Their shoes echoed in the empty building as they passed the workbenches and workplaces. Sharon opened the outer door carefully and peeped outside.

'It's all clear. What will you say to anyone you come across at the pub at this time of day?'

He grinned. 'That I was out on the

tiles and spent the night with a girlfriend.'

She coloured. He passed her and their bodied touched. He added, 'I'm not likely to meet anyone. I have a key, and Mildred won't be up for at least an hour yet. It gives me time to freshen up.'

Still feeling the excitement of being with him, Sharon declared, 'You can always stretch out on the mattress when you come back. I hope something happens today, though. We'll be shattered if we stay here tonight and all day tomorrow as well.'

He nodded. 'Agreed. But catching her red-handed will be worth it.'

He slipped through the door and set off. The sun was just rising and the morning air was fresh and misty. Sharon waited and watched Craig go. He turned up his collar and sauntered nonchalantly out of the yard and finally disappeared from her sight.

On her own again, she checked the recorder. As Craig had said, it showed nothing unusual. She opened the window for some fresh air and to cover the smell of the coffee. She thought about the time they'd spent together since last evening as she sipped the hot liquid. They got on well. He was a great person. She'd miss him like crazy.

Two hours later, he was back. He looked a lot fresher, and his aftershave hung in the air. He smiled and pronounced, 'Your turn! You can get something to eat, freshen up, and come back at your leisure.'

She nodded. 'I won't be long. Then you can take a nap for a while if you like. I'm okay now.'

'Take your time. I'm fine.'

'I checked the recorder. Nothing unusual. I rewound it and restarted it.'

'Right. I'll get myself a mug of coffee.' He lifted a newspaper. 'I bought it on the way here to study the latest football forecasts.'

Sharon grabbed her bag and went. The yard was empty. She locked the door and went home to her cottage.

She had just come out of the shower when she heard her phone. Wrapping a towel round herself, she scampered downstairs and picked it up from the hall table.

'She's here!' Craig spoke quietly.

'What!'

'She's on her own. Come back as soon as you can. I can't confront her. I've no authority to do so. When you get here, go straight to Sam's section. I'll watch the recorder and join you as soon as I see you there.'

'Craig, I'm not dressed and my hair is wet. I've just come out of the shower!'

'My dear girl, do you think that matters right now? Come back here on the double. Who knows how long she'll be around.'

Sharon pulled herself together. 'You're right; I'll come as fast as I can. I hope she doesn't do a bunk before I arrive.'

'I hope so too!'

She hurried to dress in jeans and a T-shirt, wrapped a scarf around her head, and searched frantically for her car keys. The roads were still deserted when she parked her Mini around the corner from the factory. She wondered briefly how she'd confront Sandra if she met her coming out, but it didn't happen.

She closed the entrance door and quietly re-locked it behind her, then took off her shoes and padded through the empty workrooms. She could already hear sounds before she reached Sam's section. Sandra had left the door open, so Sharon could enter without the woman noticing anything was amiss. She hoped Craig had seen her and was on the way.

When she entered, Sharon saw three small bundles in bubble wrap on the side of the desk. Sandra was tapping away at the keyboard but became suddenly aware there was someone else present. When she saw Sharon, the shock was plastered all over her face. After a second or two, she calmed down and said, 'Sharon! What are you doing here?'

'What am *I* doing here? I think I should ask you that. Actually, I can guess why.'

Blustering, Sandra exclaimed, 'I came in to help. I noticed that Sam was behind with his records and I wanted to get them up to date before he got into trouble.'

'Stop lying, Sandra. You're stealing from the company, and not for the first time either.'

Sandra's eyes narrowed. 'Stealing? How dare you! I came in to help a fellow worker.'

'I think Sam would be very surprised to hear about your concern. How did you get in? And what's that on the desk?'

'I don't know. When I arrived the parcel was already there.'

'I don't believe you. Explain how you got in.'

Awkwardly she replied, 'I had to work overtime one weekend when I first started in the factory and Gaynor gave me the key.'

'And you made a copy?'

Looking more brazen, she answered, 'Why not? I was sure I'd need to come again in the future, and I didn't want to run to Gaynor and explain. She expected me to sign for it every time. That got on my nerves.'

Looking at the computer, Sharon asked, 'Even if I believed you, why are you using Sam's computer?'

'I told you. I want to help Sam and get his records up to date.'

'Assuming I believe that, which I don't, you need his password. Where did you get it?'

Sandra pointed to the top corner of a desk calendar on the desk. 'It's there. I noticed that Sam always looked at it when he started the computer. People are more forgetful the older they get.'

Sharon took a step forward and picked up one of the packages. She unwrapped it. It contained a cup belonging to the suspected series. Sandra watched her and remained silent. Holding it, Sharon declared,

'Let's not pretend anymore, Sandra. You're stealing, and have been for a while. You've been clever enough to manipulate the records as you went along so that no one noticed for a while, but you must have realized that you'd be caught one day.'

The colour was now high in Sandra's face. She pulled an angry expression. 'When it comes down to brass tacks, Sharon, it's your word against mine, isn't it? No one else has seen me coming or going. How do you intend to prove anything?'

'Because we've been filming this area for a while. We filmed you the last couple of times you stole something. The first time your face wasn't clear, but you were wearing the same sweatshirt with the hood up as you're wearing today. The next time no one would doubt it was you. This morning it's again beyond doubt. You've been filmed since you arrived. We're being filmed at this moment.'

'And where's this camera?'

Sharon pointed to where the camera was half-hidden between the files.

Sandra made to grab it, but she was cut off mid-air when Craig caught her arm from behind. 'Not so fast. It won't do you any good to get rid of that. The recording isn't in the camera itself.' He dropped her arm and she stepped back. Craig blocked the passage to the door.

'So . . . so what are you going to do?' Her expression was less aggressive and her eyes were shifting from Craig to Sharon.

'We could call the police,' Sharon said, 'but I want to know who's behind all this. Tell us, and it might make the difference between a probationary sentence or one in jail.'

Sandra crossed her arms. 'And that's supposed to be a reasonable alternative?'

Sharon shrugged. 'It's the best we can do. We won't employ you anymore, whatever happens. If we charge you with theft and you do end up in jail, you'll have a hard job finding any work in the potteries again. Cooperate, and you may find work again in another factory as long as they don't expect a written recommendation from us. I'm not prepared to give you one under any circumstance.'

Sandra tossed her blond hair and nodded at Craig. 'What's he got to do with all of this?'

'Craig helped me set up the camera, and he's my witness to what happened here this morning.'

'Huh! Looks more like you're hard up for a boyfriend and can't get him any other way.'

Sharon's colour heightened. 'Craig was the first to notice the discrepancies, and he suggested using a camera to catch the culprit. His idea was excellent and it's worked. What do you want to do? We can call the police straight away, or you can tell us who your accomplice is and we'll decide what to do after.'

Biting her lips, Sandra stared at them angrily. 'He'll kill me!'

Craig drawled, 'Forget the dramatics.

He's not likely to kill you over a bit of china, whoever he is. Come on Sandra, out with it. Who put you up to it?'

Staring at the packages still lying on the desk, she was quiet, and then said, 'Ray, it's Ray!'

Sharon couldn't believe it. 'Ray? Our accountant? Why would he be interested in stolen china? Why would he get involved in something like this?'

'Ray has an expensive lifestyle,' she boasted. 'We've been together for a while now. He got the idea because he has a friend who has a wholesale warehouse in Leeds. Among other things, this chap buys expensive china from various companies. Ray figured we could supply him with some from here cheaper, and we could pocket money without anyone noticing. When I told him I had a key to the place, he decided it'd be a pushover. I watched Sam and how he records the incoming and outgoing items. Ray told me how to adjust production figures too. I found that password in Gaynor's desk.'

'But . . . but Ray undoubtedly earns good money, and you're one of our most highly paid painters. Why did you agree to do such a thing?'

'You wouldn't understand. You've got a house and a car. I can't afford them and never will. Ray loves expensive cars and fancy restaurants. I don't know what he earns, whether it's a lot or not, but I do know it's never enough. Anyway, I like Ray. We get on like a house on fire.'

Craig asked, 'How much did he get for the china?'

'I don't know. Ray fixed that.' Almost boasting again, she added, 'When I see what our china costs in the shops, and calculate what we've passed on to the warehouse, it must be thousands.'

Craig added, 'But you carry the whole risk. You did all the stealing and he did all the sweet-talking. Perhaps he told the warehouse owner he was getting special rates because he was the company's tax adviser.'

'And what happens now?' Sandra

asked, beginning to sound concerned.

Craig glanced at Sharon, who asked, 'What do you suggest?'

'I think we'll have to confront Ray, don't you?'

'And what about me?' Sandra looked worried.

Craig told her, 'You'll go home now. Don't think about trying to run off. We have the evidence on camera and I'm prepared to act as a witness. Once we've spoken to Ray, Miss Vaughan will contact you again and tell you what we've decided.'

She nodded, looking downhearted and nervous.

Sharon said, 'Give me the key and go. Don't mention this to your parents yet. Your future depends on how you co-operate with us.'

Sandra reached into her pocket and handed Sharon the key.

'If you have anything of importance in your locker, take it with you now. You're not coming back into the factory again, for any reason — and don't warn

Ray. If you do that, it'll make things worse for you. Whatever happens, you're finished in this factory. I know where you live. I'll be in touch.'

Craig stood aside and Sandra scuttled out. He shook his head. 'Why are people so idiotic? I can understand if they want more money; but if she wanted it for a car, a temporary extra weekend job would boost her savings. There's always a legal way, even though it takes longer. I think we should corner this chap straight away. I'm not sure whether or not Sandra will warn him. She must be potty about him to let him use her like this.'

Sharon went after Sandra to open and then re-lock the outer door. When she returned she asked, 'Do I have time to dry my hair?'

He grinned. 'I don't suppose Ray will care much what you look like when he knows why we've come. What are you planning to tell him?'

She bit her lip. 'I should threaten him with the police straight off, but I want to hear his explanation first.'

'Come on, then. Let's get it over with. Do you know where he lives?'

'He gave me his visiting card once. His private address is on that.'

'He'll need new visiting cards after this. Do you have it to hand?'

'It's in my desk.'

'Right, then get it. I suggest we take my car.'

Sharon hurried upstairs and found the card, and they were soon on their way.

12

Ray's flat was in a large converted Victorian house in the more affluent area of the next town. The street was lined with old chestnut trees, and their leaves were beginning to change colour.

As they walked up the brick pathway to the house, Craig commented, 'He's doing well for an accountant in a small firm. This is clearly an expensive area.'

Climbing the wide steps, Sharon nodded. She studied the nameplate. 'There he is — Raymond Keyes.' She pressed the button. After a few seconds, she pressed it again.

A sleepy, annoyed-sounding voice responded, 'Who is it? What do you want?'

'Sharon Vaughan. Can I have a word with you?'

His voice brightened. 'What an

unexpected surprise. Come on up. Second floor.'

There was a buzz and Sharon pushed the door open. Craig followed. They went across the tiled hallway and up the elegant stairway to the second floor. The door straight ahead was ajar. She glanced at Craig before she pushed it open and walked inside.

Out of sight, Ray shouted, 'Straight ahead! Help yourself to a drink. I'll be with you in minute.'

Sharon and Craig walked across the sparsely furnished hall displaying an expensive Persian carpet and impressive antiques. The living room faced the main road; it had two bay windows and was painted in subdued colours. Modern, exclusive furniture was placed advantageously, and the room had an expensive, very stylish atmosphere.

Craig looked around and whistled softly. 'Not bad! The furniture must have cost a bomb.'

Sharon sniffed. 'I expect he bought it with our money.'

When Ray breezed in, he paused to see Craig with Sharon, but he recovered quickly and smiled. He was dressed in designer jeans and a white shirt, and had even gone to the trouble of shaving.

'What can I do for you, Sharon? It's a pleasure to see you; but as you've brought company with you, I presume this is not a personal visit?'

'No. This is Craig Baines.'

Ray nodded in his direction. 'Yes, I know. We've already met.'

With heightened colour Sharon, continued, 'We're here to talk about Sandra stealing from the factory and your part in it.'

His eyes narrowed and the skin on his cheeks tightened, but he was quick off the mark. 'Sandra? Yes, I know Sandra, but I don't know what you're talking about. She and I have been stealing? Are you mad?'

'Come off it, Ray,' Sharon admonished him. 'Stop pretending. We caught her red-handed this morning. We've been filming the despatch area for a while. She's been caught on camera three times, and she's admitted to what she's done. She says you passed the items on to a wholesale dealer. In fact, she says you thought the whole thing up in the first place.'

Ray thrust his hands into the pockets of his jeans, and his colour rose. 'Do I look like someone who deals in stolen goods?'

Sharon met his glance straight on. 'I think you know that better than I do! You two weren't just stealing; you were clever enough to adjust our records so that no one noticed until Craig showed up. Sandra told us you were her partner, so I presume you told her exactly how to manipulate the computer once she'd obtained the passwords.'

He began to bluster. 'What proof do you have that I'm involved? It's her word against mine.'

'Don't be a worm as well as a criminal. Don't let her carry the whole can.' Sharon looked around. 'You lead a very extravagant lifestyle. Where does the money come from for you to buy an expensive car and costly antiques, and rent a flat in the most exclusive area of town? You almost certainly earn more than average, but is it enough to live the way you do?'

'It's none of your business. Perhaps I inherited money, or won it on the races or at the casino.'

'I think that if the police checked your bank account, they'd more likely find that you bought things for your flat concurrent with dates when our china was stolen. Sandra is scared of going to jail and ultimately she'll save her own skin. I'd advise you to do the same.'

Sticking his chin out, he asked, 'Why should I? A confession to anything now will guarantee a criminal charge by the police.'

'Perhaps. The only way I'll let you off the hook is if you repay us the cost of the china, resign from your present job, and move somewhere far, far away.'

Craig's eyebrows lifted. He let out a breath slowly between his teeth. 'Is that a good idea? He'll do something just as crooked again somewhere else.'

Ray spluttered, 'Do you mind? I'm not a cheap criminal. Even though I gave in to temptation, I do realize it was a stupid thing to do.' He ran his hand down his face. 'I'd just signed the lease for this flat and I couldn't wait to furnish it properly. My friend at the warehouse had already mentioned he was open to side deals, and when I was put in charge of your account I began to see it could be an extra source of money, especially when Sandra told me she had a key to the place. That put her in a perfect position to do the pilfering.'

Craig butted in: 'You were stealing! Kids pilfer; adults steal.'

Ray glared at him. 'The temptation was too great, and I thought no one would ever notice. I am ultimately responsible for balancing your accounts and could cover any irregularities quite easily. I thought it a godsend. I didn't intend for it to go on forever; just until I'd finished furnishing the flat.'

'I find that hard to believe,' Sharon said. 'You shouldn't have started in the first place, and you definitely shouldn't have dragged Sandra into your schemes either.'

'Sandra got her share of the money.'

'She should have used her intelligence to resist stealing from a company who paid her regular wage.'

'What . . . what do you intend to do?'

'That depends on you. I already sense that Craig doesn't want to give you another chance, but I'm also aware that it'll take ages until the case gets to court; and in the end they're quite likely to give both of you probationary sentences for stealing thousands of pounds worth of goods, and we won't get our money back. I also know it will ruin your lives. I'm offering you an alternative. Pay back what you've stolen down to the last penny, and move away.'

He was silent for a short time, then he nodded quickly. 'I've kept exact records of all the china we gave the wholesaler. I'll find a way of repaying you the money.' He gestured around. 'Most likely I'll have to sell nearly all of this stuff. Provided you're satisfied with that, I'm prepared to start looking for a job down south straight away. I've always fancied working in London. I'll need time to find something.'

'I want a list of what you stole now. I bet your accounting training automatically means you kept a list of everything. I also want a written statement from you admitting that you sold stolen goods in partnership with Sandra. When you've repaid the amount, and proved you're moving away to another job, you'll get the statement back. I'll give you two months at the most to find something. Otherwise, I'll go to the police with your statement and have you both charged.'

Ray studied her briefly. 'You're very pretty, but you're cut glass when it comes to business, aren't you? Okay — and I realize you're being fair under the circumstances — I'll never do anything as stupid again. I was carried away because it all seemed so easy.'

Sharon adjusted the strap of her bag. 'Just give me the list and a written statement and we'll be off. Don't keep us hanging around, or I might change my mind.'

He nodded silently. 'Be back in a minute.'

He hurried off, and Craig gave her a sideways glance, his head tipped to one side. 'I don't know if this is a sensible move. Most people would have handed them both over to the police.'

Sharon shrugged. 'I know. Perhaps it's daft, but I want the money back.' She paused. 'We'll have to search for a replacement for Sandra. Perhaps we ought to train apprentices. People are always going to leave; and without trained replacements, disruption will be inevitable.'

Craig threw back his head and laughed out loud. 'You're unbelievable.' His expression steadied again. 'Do you know when Granville is putting his shares up for sale?'

'Oh yes — Granville! Good that you

reminded me. I'll have to tell him about developments. Now that he's pulling out of the company, I don't think he actually cares about how I handle things. That's fine by me, because I hate quarrelling. I think the shares will be on offer soon.'

'Right.' Craig retained his affability, but Sharon thought she noticed a hardening of his eyes.

'I don't think he'll hang on much longer,' she said. 'He told me recently he needs money for the stable conversions. I'll buy as many shares as I can afford and hope the firm stays afloat. I also hope that any new investors are just in it for the money. If strangers demand a say in how I manage things, it'll be hell.'

Ray came back with some sheets of paper. 'Is this okay?'

A shadow of annoyance crossed Sharon's face as she checked his list and glanced at his admission. She handed them to Craig to read. He frowned as he read them, and finally nodded.

Sharon remarked sharply, 'Okay, that's it. Don't forget, Ray — don't drag your feet, and no tricks.' She turned on her heel. Craig gave Ray a hostile look before he started to follow her out.

Ray said quickly, 'By the way, why are you wearing a scarf? It's most unbecoming.'

Sharon's colour heightened. She didn't reply. Craig grinned as he closed the door behind them.

Outside on the way to his car, a snazzy BMW, Craig asked, 'And what now? Back to the village to rescue your hair?'

Sharon glared. 'Don't you start! I would've preferred to face him looking like the Fairy Princess, but fate decided otherwise.'

He grinned. 'How you look hasn't made any difference to the outcome, has it?'

Grumpily she replied, 'True. But I don't like being caught on the wrong foot. I look like one of Granville's horsey friends.'

Fixing his belt, he remarked, 'So, back to the village?'

She slipped into the passenger seat and struggled to fit the seat-belt tongue into its slot. She hadn't realized how glad she was that the confrontation was over. She also wished Craig was remaining in her life instead of moving on to his next task. Looking out, she paused and then said, 'Yes, and then I suppose I'd better inform Granville. He's still officially chairman of the board.'

Craig stared stiffly ahead. 'Yes, I suppose you're right.'

'Drop me off at my cottage, and once I've dried my hair I'll go to see him.'

'His place is on our way back, isn't it? Can you cope with facing him in your headscarf? I don't mind making a slight detour.'

'That would be great. I'll make it as brief as I can. And stop referring to my headscarf.' She tossed her head. 'It's real silk!'

Each of them was busy with their

own thoughts until Craig halted outside Granville's manor house.

★ ★ ★

Granville was coming down the entrance steps dressed in a tweed jacket with elbow patches, a red setter at his heels. He came towards the car, opened Sharon's door and held out a hand to help her out, then kissed her cheek. 'What a pleasant surprise.' He looked at Craig. 'What brings the two of you here this afternoon?'

Sharon hurried to explain. 'There are new developments regarding the theft at the factory. Have you a moment to spare? I'd like to put you in the picture.'

'Of course. Come in! I'll ask Mrs Dawson to get us some tea.' He turned to lead the way.

Sharon looked at Craig. 'Come with me. You're just as involved.'

Granville looked back over his shoulder. 'Yes, do come, old chap. Sharon's told me how much you

253

helped. There's no point in you sitting out here on your own. Not the thing at all.'

Looking unperturbed, Craig followed, and Granville led the way to the library. He asked again, 'Tea?'

Sharon shook her head and looked at Craig. 'You, Craig?'

'No thanks.'

'Yes, well, sit down and tell me what's going on.'

A few minutes later Granville was up to date. He was surprised but satisfied. 'You seem to have everything under control. I suppose I should argue with you about giving both of them a second chance, but as I won't be in charge of the company in the future, I'll string along. The main thing is that they return the money. If that man doesn't keep his word, I'll have a word with his boss. That'll cook his goose.'

Sharon nodded. 'Agreed.'

'What makes someone who's had long professional training go bad like that?'

Craig shifted in the leather chair. 'The temptation of money! Especially when you know how to avoid detection and someone else does the dirty work. He enjoys living beyond his means.'

Granville nodded. Sharon was glad they'd come. Now she just had to make sure that Sandra and Ray kept the agreement. She asked, 'Have you put your shares up for sale yet?'

He smiled at her and shoved some blond hair off his forehead. 'No, but they'll be on offer at the beginning of the week.'

She bit her lip. 'I just hope we don't end up with owners who strangle us with their interference.'

Trying to lighten the atmosphere, he pointed out, 'I don't think you need to worry. When Craig's report is public, they'll read that you've got everything under control and they won't need to interfere.'

Sharon got up and Craig followed. 'Well, thanks for your time,' she said.

'Hope we haven't interrupted something important?'

'No; I was just on my way to the architect. He's drawn up initial plans and wants to go ahead and get building permission. I'll phone you when the foundations are laid. You must come and meet everyone.'

Granville led the way out. Craig overtook the other two. When he was in the driver's seat, he looked in the rear mirror and saw Granville give Sharon a farewell kiss on her cheek before she hurried to join him. His jaw was clenched and he drove off with excessive speed, shooting the gravel in all directions as they travelled down the driveway.

Now that the pottery's problems were working out at last, Sharon couldn't ignore her own confusion anymore. She prayed she wouldn't give herself away until after Craig had left. Then she'd channel all her efforts into her work and somehow find a way to get on with her life again.

13

On Monday morning, Sharon grabbed
Gaynor as soon as she arrived and told
her about Sandra and Ray, then asked
her not to tell anyone else. At the
moment, the official version was that
Sandra had left of her own accord. It
would be early enough to tell everyone
the whole truth if Sandra and Ray
didn't keep their side of the bargain. 'I
didn't want to keep you in the dark, but
I had to be absolutely fair and treat
everyone equally.'

Gaynor looked a little disappointed,
but it was only temporary. She brightened and nodded. 'Of course; I understand.
You couldn't afford to show any favour-
itism, could you? But I'm shocked! Mind
you, I don't have much in common with
Sandra. She only ever seemed to talk
about clothes, dieting, her latest boyfriends, and having fun.'

Sharon nodded. 'In many ways, it's a great shame. She's a talented painter and we'll miss her.'

Gaynor's lips pursed. 'We won't miss someone who steals from the hand that feeds her.'

Sharon was glad to get back to work again. Mid-morning she went to give Gaynor some work and looked across, hoping to see Craig, but his office was empty. 'Where is he?' she asked.

'Around somewhere, clearing up loose ends. He mentioned that he's finishing at the end of the week.'

'Is he? I didn't realize that.' Sharon's heart plunged.

Her bank manager phoned on Wednesday to tell her the company shares were on the market and to check that he should bid for ten percent of them, as she'd arranged. She told him to go ahead. Sipping a coffee with Gaynor later, she told her about Granville's withdrawal from the company and what it might mean for them all.

'I can't afford to buy more than I have already. Heaven help us! It might mean an upheaval if we end up with someone who's a nit-picker or busybody as the main shareholder. Let's hope for the best.'

Facing Craig's imminent departure bothered her even more than the fate of the company. She hoped she wouldn't give herself away when he said goodbye. She loved him so much it hurt just thinking about never seeing him again.

★   ★   ★

On Friday, Gaynor bought éclairs and made coffee while Craig said his goodbyes to various people he'd got to know downstairs. Then he came back upstairs to clear his desk and join the others in the office.

Sharon forced a smile and gripped her mug tightly. She felt ice spreading through her stomach thinking that it was just minutes before he left. 'We'll miss you, Craig, even though we branded you as our opponent when you arrived.'

'Will you?' He eyed her carefully. 'I hope so. You labelled me as trouble with a big T. Gaynor was a lot more welcoming.'

She swallowed hard. 'Granville told me your report is positive. Thank you for that.'

He held her glance. 'Don't thank me. I report what I find. I never let personal issues colour my work.'

Sharon took a hasty sip of her coffee.

Gaynor asked, 'When are you leaving? Where are you going?'

He shrugged. 'First thing tomorrow morning. I'll find out where the next assignment is when I go to the office on Monday.'

Gaynor nodded. 'Circumstances change continually, don't they? Just think of what's happened here since you arrived. The thieving, Granville selling his shares, you coming and going . . . who knows what's next? Perhaps the next chairman will make our lives hell.'

He smiled. 'I don't think so. You'll find out eventually anyway, but I can reassure you on that point, I bought up the rest of the available shares.'

'What!' Sharon squealed and spilt her coffee. 'You? Why?'

His eyes sparkled as he viewed her consternation. 'Because I think the company is a going concern and that my money is well-invested.'

'But . . . but isn't it unethical? You've just written a report about us.'

'I'd finished my report and presented it before Granville put his shares on offer, so I no longer have any professional connections. I asked my boss whether or not I was allowed to do so under the circumstances. He checked for me, and it was.'

Gaynor beamed. 'That's great. Not just because we already know you, but because you know the company. We'll see you at board meetings.'

Feeling bewildered, Sharon was calm enough to say, 'Craig doesn't have to attend. He can name a surrogate.'

'True,' Craig agreed. 'But I'll call a meeting of all shareholders to discuss the new structure.'

Sharon stared at him. He met her glance. 'As I own the majority of shares, I hope to be elected chairman. And as you now own twenty percent, that means together we can overrule any problems the others make. I'll propose that we make you managing director. I'll attend meetings as often as I can, and keep in touch.'

The telephone rang and Gaynor grabbed it. Looking annoyed, she declared, 'Okay, I'll come — but if Colin's mixed up the delivery orders again, he'll get the sharp edge of my tongue.' She slammed the phone down and hurried out.

Left alone, Sharon stared at Craig for a moment. 'Why did you do it?' she asked him. 'It must have cost you a bomb.'

He gave her a lopsided smile. 'I sold my house and used the rest of my savings. I'll survive! I have no intention of pouring my money down the drain. The pottery is doing okay. It's a going concern.' He was briefly silent. 'Admittedly I did have a personal reason. I did it for you.'

It felt like an electric shock to her system. 'For me!'

'I know how much the company means to you.' He shifted his weight. 'If Granville loves you, I can't understand why he opted out. I felt I had to secure your position here.'

Her mouth was dry. 'You know why Granville sold the shares — he did it to finance his horse-breeding scheme. He's fallen in love with someone who gave him the idea.' She breathed deeply. 'It seems you're under some kind of wrong impression about me and Granville. I was never in love with him and told him so months ago. He thought he was in love with me, until he met his present girlfriend.'

Craig stood up and slammed his coffee mug onto the table. 'You don't love him?'

Sharon shook her head. 'He was chairman of the board, and I liked him — I *still* like him — but it never went beyond that.'

'But the rumours . . . '

'You know what village people are like. A spark is a forest fire!'

He was lost for words and struggling with himself 'And there's no one else? No other man in your life?'

Sharon was puzzled but began to hope. 'Why do you want to know?'

'Because I'd like to apply for the position. Is it free?'

She caught her breath and her hand flew to her throat. 'Don't make jokes about something so serious, Craig.'

His eyes were dark with longing. 'I've never been more serious. I've been in love with you virtually from day one. I never thought it would happen to me, but you captured my imagination body and soul. You do every time I see you.' As soon as the words left his mouth, he looked anxious that he'd torpedoed any chance he might have had with her.

Sharon was full of mounting happiness. She grinned mischievously, and then her face displayed her delight. 'Dear prospective chairman, I accept your application and offer you the position. It's full-time!'

He was clearly astonished. His gaze roved and he studied her intently.

'What?'

Her eyes were bright, her voice buoyant. 'I can't imagine coming to work and not finding you here. I can't imagine not seeing you again. I never thought I'd fall in love either, but I have.' She took a hesitant step forward, and he pulled her into his arms. She could feel his heart thudding against her own. With a giddy sense of pleasure, she could finally let her happiness show.

His mouth covered hers hungrily. Sharon wrapped her arms around him and slipped her hands inside his collar. Her heart was still thumping nineteen to the dozen as they drew apart and gazed at each other. Then his lips recaptured hers, and were more demanding. Her thoughts were scattered and she was too excited to think straight.

'So we've both been pretending, avoiding each other, and wasting time?' he breathed. 'I noticed you were keeping your distance.'

'I had to because I didn't want a fleeting affair. I thought you were just passing through. It looks like I was wrong about a few things.' Her emotions whirled and skidded as she relaxed and enjoyed the feel of his arms around her. When she looked up, his gaze met hers, and her heart did a jig.

His grin flashed briefly. 'I'm so glad about that.' His gaze travelled over her face and then met her eyes. 'I can't believe this. I was wondering how I could leave this place, and you, without falling apart. Now I need to figure out how to change my plans and stay here.'

She chuckled. 'You've sold your house and burned your boats down south.'

His whole face spread into a smile.

'From now on I want my home wherever you are.'

With her pulse pounding noticeably, she sighed and with raised eyebrows she managed to ask, 'And what about your next commission? What if they want to send you to Scotland or Cornwall?'

'To hell with my next commission.' He laughed, and it boomed through the room. 'I've already played with the idea of going independent several times. Now that I know you're keen on me, and knowing that I can't tempt you away from this place, I'll find a way to stay here. I'll start up my own business!'

She blinked. 'Just like that?' He smiled, and Sharon sensed his dynamism and how irresistible he was. Knowing that he cared for her was a new and overwhelming feeling. If he told her he was organizing a Sunday outing to Mars, and she should come along, she would go.

He said, 'Why not? Small businesses need the same advice as international ones. I could concentrate on local enterprises.'

Trying to be sensible, Sharon replied, 'You're right. What about your boss? How will he react?'

'We've always got on well, and I wouldn't leave him high and dry. If he's scheduled me on another job already, I'll have to do it, but then he'll have to agree to my leaving. It'd only be for another couple of weeks, and I'd definitely spend every weekend here.'

A smile covered Sharon's face as she asked, 'If you're planning to start up your business locally, where will you live?'

He saw his future written in her smile. 'Haven't a clue. Somewhere nearby, so that I can see you every day.'

'If you give me decent references, I might take you in myself.'

A grin overtook his features and he whooped. 'You mean that?'

'It's the best way to find out if we belong together. I think it'd be an excellent solution, don't you?'

He grew silent and then kissed the tip of her nose. She buried her face in his neck. 'What if we don't get on?' he asked.

Sharon looked up again. 'Then you move out and I spend the rest of my life wondering what I did wrong.'

His eyes never leaving hers, he whispered, 'Many people walk in and out of a person's life, but only someone special leaves an imprint on their heart. You've made one on mine. I'll never let you go. I'll protect you, I'll care for you, and I promise to love you as long as I live.' He gave her a smile that melted any misgivings. He hugged her close and then kissed her in a way that left her in no doubt about their future.

Somehow Sharon knew that he was going to be part of her life forever more, and she'd never been so thankful. He was all she'd unknowingly wanted all her life. He was Craig, and amazingly he loved her and wanted to be hers.

IT'S NEVER TOO LATE
THE MOST WONDERFUL TIME
OF THE YEAR
THE SILVER LINING

We do hope that you have enjoyed reading this large print book.

Did you know that all of our titles are available for purchase?

We publish a wide range of high quality large print books including:
**Romances, Mysteries, Classics
General Fiction
Non Fiction and Westerns**

Special interest titles available in large print are:
**The Little Oxford Dictionary
Music Book, Song Book
Hymn Book, Service Book**

Also available from us courtesy of Oxford University Press:
**Young Readers' Dictionary
(large print edition)
Young Readers' Thesaurus
(large print edition)**

For further information or a free brochure, please contact us at:
**Ulverscroft Large Print Books Ltd.,
The Green, Bradgate Road, Anstey,
Leicester, LE7 7FU, England.
Tel:** (00 44) **0116 236 4325
Fax:** (00 44) **0116 234 0205**

A HEART'S WAGER

Heidi Sullivan

Eva Copperfield has lived a life of poverty in the squalid slums of New York — until a sudden inheritance gives her the chance of a new life as lady of the manor in the English countryside. Her journey from rags to riches is complicated by the mysterious Ben — who is either a lord or a charlatan! Eva has to navigate the Atlantic and her heart before she can find a home . . . and love. Wagers are being made. Who will win?

MALLORCAN MAGIC

Jill Barry

On the rebound from a broken engagement, romance is the last thing on Eira's mind as she treats herself to a holiday in Mallorca. But two chance encounters with handsome entrepreneur Danny Carpenter, followed by a job offer as his children's nanny, set her on an entirely unexpected path. Soon she must deal not only with the complicated issue of falling for her employer, but also of coming to his defence when he is arrested and taken into custody for a crime he is certainly innocent of committing . . .